"You kno... is about. That ancient man-woman thing is pulling at us so strong we can hardly fight it."

"Oh, yes, we can. I can, and I will," Kaya said. "I've had my heart broken by one Cunningham man. I'm not about to make the same mistake again."

"Did anybody ever tell you that those eyes of yours can put a spell on a man? Crack his heart in two."

"I don't think you're afraid of a broken heart."

He grinned at her roguishly. "Maybe not, but you sure can put a man's body into a lot of torment. And if you're truthful, you won't deny that you feel that electric force between us, too."

"I don't deny it, but that doesn't mean I'll give in to it. No way. Never."

"Never say never."

"I bet you never risked your heart, did you?"

An expression she couldn't interpret crossed his face.

Dear Reader,

Whether you're enjoying one of the first snowfalls of the season or lounging in a beach chair at some plush island resort, I hope you've got some great books by your side. I'm especially excited about the Silhouette Romance titles this month as we're kicking off 2006 with two great new miniseries by some of your all-time favorite authors.

Cara Colter teams up with her daughter, Cassidy Caron, to launch our new PERPETUALLY YOURS trilogy. *In Love's Nine Lives* (#1798) a beautiful librarian's extremely possessive tabby tries to thwart a budding romance between *his* mistress and a man who seems all wrong for her but is anything but. Teresa Southwick returns with *That Touch of Pink* (#1799)—the first in her BUY-A-GUY trilogy. When a single mom literally buys a former military man at a bachelor auction to help her daughter earn a wilderness badge, she gets a lot more than she bargained for...and is soon earning points toward *her own* romantic survival badge. Old sparks turn into an all-out blaze when the hero returns to the family ranch in *Sometimes When We Kiss* (#1800) by Linda Goodnight. Finally, Elise Mayr debuts with *The Rancher's Redemption* (#1801) in which a widow, desperate to help her sick daughter, throws herself on the mercy of her commanding brother-in-law whose eyes reflect anything but the hate she'd expected.

And be sure to come back next month for more great reading, with Sandra Paul's distinctive addition to the PERPETUALLY YOURS trilogy and Judy Christenberry's new madcap mystery.

Have a very happy and healthy 2006.

Ann Leslie Tuttle
Associate Senior Editor

Please address questions and book requests to:
Silhouette Reader Service
U.S.: 3010 Walden Ave., P.O. Box 1325, Buffalo, NY 14269
Canadian: P.O. Box 609, Fort Erie, Ont. L2A 5X3

THE
RANCHER'S
REDEMPTION
ELISE MAYR

SILHOUETTE **Romance** ®

Published by Silhouette Books

America's Publisher of Contemporary Romance

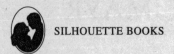 **SILHOUETTE BOOKS**

ISBN 0-373-19801-9

THE RANCHER'S REDEMPTION

Copyright © 2006 by Elise Mayr

Printed in U.S.A.

ELISE MAYR

started to read early—and didn't stop, not even when she switched languages from her native Austrian/German to English. Having spent her happiest hours with books, she knew early on that her life's work would center on them. She became a school librarian and for a quarter of a century devoted herself to instilling a love of reading in children. Eventually this love extended to writing. When not writing fiction, Elise likes to travel, tend her flower garden and take care of the pets that share their lives with her and her husband. Readers may contact her on the Web at elisemayr@aol.com.

To Ardys, who first introduced me to romances.

Chapter One

"Stop!"

For an instant Kaya Cunningham wondered if she could make it to the private elevator only ten feet away. In the security mirror mounted high on the wall she caught an image of the guard rushing toward her. Even though the image was distorted by the curved mirror, she could tell that his hand rested on the gun strapped to his hip. Defeat surged through her. She had come so close.

"Young lady, where in tarnation do you think you're goin'? Didn't you see all the signs warning you that this here was a private area?" His eyes narrowed in suspicion. "Didn't I see you in this building yesterday?" he demanded.

"Yes. I have to see Joshua Cunningham."

"You got an appointment?"

"No."

"Then I'm sorry, miss. You can't go up there without an appointment."

"But I have to see him! This is really important." Some of her desperation must have come through in her voice, because the guard's expression softened. Pleadingly she added, "I know this sounds like a cliché, but it really is a matter of life and death." Thinking of that small body lying in the hospital bed, Kaya lifted her hands in a gesture of mute supplication. "Please," she murmured, tears gathering in her eyes.

The guard cleared his throat. He avoided her eyes as if her emotional appeal embarrassed him. He probably thought she was one of Joshua Cunningham's women who had gotten the brush-off.

"Please," she said again. "I won't tell how I got up to the private floor. I won't get you into trouble. I promise I won't."

"Won't do you no good to go up there. He ain't there."

"But I was told he was!" she cried out, disappointment surging through her.

"He was, but he left a half hour ago." Glancing cautiously around him, the guard added in a low voice, "Seems to me I overheard somebody say he went back to the Diamond C. But you didn't get that from me!"

"No, I didn't. Thanks." Kaya flashed him a grateful smile and hurried out of the modern office building with the discreet plaque beside the front door identifying it as the Cunningham Tower.

The ranch. That made sense. Unlike some of the Cunninghams, Joshua had always preferred to spend his time there. Of course, that was before he became the head honcho of Cunningham Enterprises. Six years ago, when she had spent a few heaven-and-hell months on the Diamond C, he had been an honest-to-goodness cowboy, getting up at dawn, riding out with the men, not to return until evening, all sweaty and tired. Though his cool blue eyes and cynical smile had left her tongue-tied in his presence, Kaya had admired him for working so hard when he didn't have to.

The ranch was a long way from Abilene. Before she started the trip, she would stop at the hospital to see Natalie.

Even though it was hours until visiting time started, Sister Margaret pretended not to see Kaya as she headed toward her daughter's room. Kaya paused outside the door long enough to fix a cheerful smile onto her face. She heard the sounds of Saturday morning cartoons even before she entered the room.

Natalie lay on her back, her eyes closed. Not watching her favorite cartoon meant that her headache had started even earlier than usual. Kaya bit her lower lip to stifle the sob that rose in her throat. She had to be strong and cheerful and optimistic. As soon as she sat on the edge of her daughter's bed, the girl's eyelids fluttered open. The deep blue eyes lit up when she saw her mother.

"Hi, sweetie. How are you this morning?" Kaya stroked her daughter's silken brown hair.

"I'm okay, Mommy."

What a plucky little liar she was, Kaya thought, love squeezing her heart.

"Natalie, I have to drive to a ranch to speak to someone. I probably won't get back to see you tonight. Can you handle that?"

"A real ranch? With horses and cowboys and everything?" Natalie asked, perking up.

Kaya smiled. "Yes, with horses and cowboys and everything."

"Maybe you can take me there when I'm better. Maybe I could ride one of the horses. Wouldn't that be fun?"

"Yes, it would. We'll see. Have you had your medication yet?"

"I'm just bringing it," Sister Margaret announced, entering the room.

"I stopped by to tell Natalie that I had to make a short trip and probably won't be back before evening visiting hours are over," Kaya explained with a worried expression.

"That's okay. Natalie's a big girl. We can manage a few hours without your mom, can't we, honey?" Sister Margaret smiled fondly at the little girl.

"Sure," Natalie said, her voice brave. "I'm almost five."

Kaya kissed her daughter's pale cheek. "I'll see you tomorrow then." It nearly broke her heart to leave the little girl lying there, sick and alone, struck again by a persistent, debilitating anemia, but Kaya had no choice. She could no longer take care of Natalie by herself. As bitter as it was to admit, she needed help now.

Heading southeast out of Abilene, Kaya rehearsed what she would say to Joshua Cunningham. No matter what words she chose, she ended up pleading for money. She, who had never begged for anything in her life no matter how hard times were, was reduced to begging now. But then, her daughter's life had never been at stake before. For Natalie she would beg, bargain and dance with the devil himself.

Though it had been nearly six years since she had driven to the Diamond C, she had no trouble finding the famous ranch. When she brought her compact car to a stop before the front porch, she heard the sound of the triangle, summoning the hands to supper.

Kaya slid out of the driver's seat. Her body felt stiff from the long drive. The wrist she had broken earlier that year in a fall ached the way it always did just before it rained.

Automatically she rubbed it. She took a deep breath before she gathered her courage and walked to the door.

What if Lily Cunningham was in residence? The mere thought of facing her former mother-in-law caused Kaya's mouth to dry up faster than a west Texas creek in mid-August. Lily made the Wicked Witch of the West look like a benign fairy godmother, but thinking of Natalie in that hospital bed gave Kaya the courage to ring the doorbell.

The house looked the same today as it had the day she had left it, her heart broken, her will to live almost nonexistent. She heard footsteps on the other side of the door and steeled herself. When Kaya saw the elderly cowboy, she expelled the breath she had been holding. "Hi, Clancy. I don't know if you remember me—"

"'Course I do, Miss Kaya, even though I ain't laid eyes on you since before your husband was killed. Never had the chance to tell you how sorry I was about Derrick."

"Thank you," Kaya murmured.

"Well, heck. Where are my manners? Come on in."

"Is Lily here?"

Clancy snorted. "If her highness was visitin', you think I'd be allowed past the kitchen? Heck no. Four years ago Lily took her fancy French cook and her maid and moved to Dallas." Clancy grinned happily. "And none of us is sorry neither that she hardly ever comes back," he confided with a wink.

"Is Joshua here?"

"Yup. Got back a while ago from town, but when he heard one of the horses was sick, he went down to the stable. I expect he'll be back directly. Come to the kitchen. I got pies in the oven I need to tend to."

Kaya followed Clancy to the kitchen. His limp, the result of a fall from a bucking horse, seemed more pronounced than it had been, but other than that, he looked the same as the last time she'd seen him.

The huge kitchen was fragrant with apples and cinnamon. Clancy took two golden-crusted pies out of the oven and set them on the counter next to the ones already cooling there.

"I gotta take them pies down to the bunkhouse. All except one. Josh still has a sweet tooth." Clancy placed three pies on a tray.

He was the only one who ever referred to Joshua Cunningham as Josh. No one else dared. And that was as it should be, for there was nothing diminutive about the man. Not only was he physically large, he had a courageous spirit and a generous heart—at least toward those who were loyal to him.

Joshua Cunningham had taken over the Diamond C when he was in his early twenties, at a time when his father had just been diagnosed with cancer and the ranch was in serious financial trouble. It had taken years of hard work, but Joshua managed to put the Diamond C back on a self-supporting basis.

"You want some coffee, Miss Kaya?"

"Yes, thank you."

"Help yourself," he said, nodding toward the plugged in coffeemaker.

Kaya held the back door open for Clancy. Then she poured herself a cup of coffee. Leaning against the sink, she sipped the strong, bitter brew. She needed the stimulation of the coffee. The long drive, the short nights since Natalie had gotten ill, and the constant worry, suddenly had her feeling exhausted.

She had taken no more than three or four sips when she heard footsteps approaching the kitchen. Kaya didn't have to see the person to know to whom the determined steps belonged. She stood up straight though her knees trembled and her heart seemed to have jumped up into her throat.

When Joshua saw her, he stopped dead in his tracks, staring at her with his intense blue eyes as if she were a ghost. If anyone had told her that Joshua Cunningham could be rendered speechless, she wouldn't have believed them. Until that instant.

He was still wearing a gray suit, though he had loosened his red-striped tie and undone the top button of his crisply starched white shirt. He looked every inch the successful businessman. Successful Texas businessman, she amended, when she noted that he wore black cowboy boots. Kaya had to remind herself that as heir to the Cunningham holdings, that's what he was now. She was so used to remembering him looking like a working cowboy, that this new corporate executive image temporarily threw her into confusion. She couldn't remember a word of the speech she had rehearsed.

"My God," Joshua finally said, his voice filled with disbelief. "I'd have sooner expected to see Julia Roberts in my kitchen than you."

She managed a small, rueful smile before she spoke. "Believe me, I never expected to be in your kitchen again, either."

"The way you ran out on Derrick, I'd think this is the last place on earth you'd like to be."

Kaya's smile died. "I didn't run out on Derrick."

A frown deepened the lines between Joshua's eyebrows. "Oh, no? How would you describe your departure?"

"Not being asked to stay."

"Is there a difference?"

"A big difference."

With a dismissing gesture he said, "Word games." He slipped out of his suit jacket and draped it over the back of the nearest kitchen chair. "I could use a drink. How about you?"

"Coffee's fine for me."

"I'd forgotten that you never indulged. Still don't, huh?"

"I don't see any point in drinking alcohol when I don't like the taste." And couldn't afford it, she added silently. "Besides, back then, I was only seventeen, too young to drink legally. Not that Derrick let that stop him."

Joshua grimaced. "Yeah. As soon as he got his driver's license he thought he should be able to do whatever a grown man could do."

And none of you told him that he couldn't. Kaya badly wanted to utter the words, but arguing with Joshua wouldn't get her the financial help she needed. Derrick died a long time ago, but his daughter lived. Thinking of Natalie, Kaya's hands tightened around the coffee mug. She waited for Joshua to speak. It was his move. She sensed all sorts of undercurrents radiating from the big man who kept glancing at her. From experience she knew that silence and patience were her best weapons.

Joshua took a bottle of bourbon from one of the kitchen cabinets and poured a small amount into a glass. He added a couple of ice cubes. Then, leaning against the counter, he studied her thoroughly, starting with her sandal-clad feet and slowly working his way up to her face. He made no attempt to hide his obvious appraisal of her. It took all of Kaya's willpower not to reveal how nervous his slow evaluation made her, but years ago she had learned the hard way that you never revealed a weakness to a Cunningham. Not if you didn't want that weakness exploited.

When his gaze reached her eyes, she asked, "Well, what's the verdict?" When he remained silent, she said, "You've had a fairly critical look at me, so let's hear it. I don't remember you being shy."

"Come on, Kaya. You know damn well what you look like. In my experience women spend enough time in front of a mirror to know exactly what their charms are."

Kaya shook her head wearily. "Maybe women like your stepmother who have nothing else to do but worry about their looks."

"What's the matter? Life been rough on you since you left the security of the Cunningham money?"

Kaya felt heat rush into her face. "For a moment I'd forgotten how cruel the Cunninghams can be."

"And I'd forgotten how thin-skinned you were. I know Lily exploited your sensitivity. Whether you believe it or not, there were times when I wanted to come to your defense, but that would only have increased my stepmother's wrath. Besides, in your own quiet way, you held your own with Lily."

Joshua's unexpectedly approving tone temporarily flustered Kaya. She vividly remembered those scenes with her mother-in-law. In the presence of visitors, Lily would call her green-eyed, black-haired daughter-in-law *exotic looking*. At other times she would throw political correctness out the window and refer to Kaya's ethnic background in unflattering terms. Even half a dozen years later, the memory still caused Kaya's heart to feel as if it were squeezed by a vise. She took a deep breath before she spoke.

"I didn't come here to discuss the past."

"No, I suppose you didn't," Joshua said, never taking his eyes off her.

Despite the tight control Kaya had wrapped around herself like a suit of armor, her hand holding the coffee cup, trembled. It was nearly impossible not to be nervous when those blue eyes of his kept taking an inventory of her. She became acutely aware of the inexpensive denim wrap skirt, plain white cotton blouse and sandals she wore. She had been briefly tempted to put on her best dress, but even her finest outfit couldn't compete with the clothes worn by the women Joshua dated. Besides, she hadn't come to the ranch to impress him.

He took a sip of bourbon before he asked, "Just why did you come, Kaya? Why now, after all these years when we didn't get so much as a Christmas card from you?"

"Lily would have tossed my Christmas card into the trash without so much as looking at it twice, so why bother? Anyway…" Kaya took another shaky breath. Here goes, she thought, her heart beating even harder.

"I tried to see you in Abilene, but your security people wouldn't let me near you. Basically I want to ask you a question."

Joshua's left eyebrow rose. "You drove all the way from Abilene to ask me a question? It must be a real beauty. Let's hear it."

Kaya's mouth was so dry she had to take a sip of coffee before she could speak. "When the Cunningham attorney presented me with the divorce petition, he also gave me a bank slip with an account number on it. Did you know that?"

Joshua nodded. "A generous offer which you proudly

tore up. What's the matter? Do you regret that impulsive, grand gesture now?"

She had heard Joshua's voice turn as softly soothing as a mild spring breeze when calming a frightened horse, but now it had turned as cold as an arctic blast. This was going to be even harder than she had feared. Ignoring his verbal jab, Kaya asked, "I realize a lot of time has passed, but do I still have access to that account?" If the question caught him off guard, he didn't show it.

"What do you want the money for?" Joshua asked, looking at his drink with a studiedly bored expression.

Kaya wasn't fooled by his disinterested pose. If only she could tell him the truth about Natalie. If he knew who her father was…too risky. She dared not tell him. As casually as she could, she asked, "Does my getting the money depend on what I need it for?"

"I can't remember if there were any stipulations or limitations attached to it, but you can't blame me for wanting to know. First you reject the settlement in a very dramatic manner, and then years later, you want it." He looked at her through narrowed eyes. "What's happened? You got a boyfriend who's short of funds? Did he find out you might have access to the Cunningham millions? Does he want to get his hands on some of that money?"

Red color flooded Kaya's face. She flung polite caution to the wind and demanded, "Why do the Cunninghams always assume the worst about me? Granted, I'm not in the social register. Nor am I wealthy. And yes, one side of my family tree includes both Native Americans as well as Hispanics, but by heaven, that doesn't make me automatically inferior, and I resent you treating me as if I were!"

"I've never—"

"Yes, you have. Just now. There could be a dozen legitimate reasons why I need the money. My car might need major repairs, or a fire could have destroyed my apartment, or I could have lost my job, but did you think of any of these reasons? No. You immediately jumped to the shabbiest possibility you could think of. You judged me. How dare you?"

Joshua leveled a hard look at Kaya. His mouth thinned. "I dare because sooner or later everybody wants something from us. If you're a Cunningham you learn at an early age that people cozy up to you only so they can use you."

"And is that what you think I'm doing? Did I ever ask any of you for a single penny of your precious money before?"

"No. But that's probably because you were too young to recognize the golden opportunity you had for taking a good chunk of the Cunningham holdings. Now you're older and wiser in the ways of the world, and perhaps you've decided to remedy that."

All Kaya could do was shake her head. She didn't trust herself to speak. She felt humiliation and desperation press in on her. If she didn't need that money so urgently for Natalie, she'd... No. She couldn't and wouldn't lose her temper. For her daughter's sake, she'd be polite if it killed her.

Tears tightened and closed off her throat. She bit the inside of her right cheek to stop the flow of tears. She would die before she cried in front of this man who so obviously disliked her. She turned her back on Joshua as she carefully set her coffee cup on the counter. Was he refusing to give her the money? He couldn't refuse her. He just couldn't. She had nowhere else to turn. Afraid of his answer, she still had to ask for it.

"Are you telling me that the account is closed?" Her

voice barely squeezed past the painful tightness in her throat.

"No, that's not what I'm telling you. I don't know if there's a time limit on the settlement."

At least this wasn't an out-and-out refusal. The relief was so great that Kaya had to clutch the edge of the sink to remain upright. The porcelain felt cool under her sweating palms. Turning to face him, she said, "If you'll give me the account number, I'll get out of your house and out of your life. I promise I won't bother you anymore."

"Running away again?" he asked, his voice taunting.

Quietly but firmly she said, "No, I'm not running away, but I don't like to be in a place where I was never welcome."

"This is my house now, not Lily's."

"And I'm still not welcome." Kaya heard the trace of bitterness in her voice and hated it. Why should she care whether Joshua Cunningham made her feel welcome or not?

He drained his drink before he spoke. "Come. Let's go to my office. That document must be somewhere in the files. I'll check for a time limit."

Kaya followed him down the hall. In the office every surface was covered with computer printouts, ledgers, old tally books, invoices, feed catalogues and receipts. How on earth could he find anything in this mess?

Seeing Kaya's expression, Joshua said, rather defensively, "This may look disorganized, but I can put my hands on whatever I need."

"You should get one of your secretaries to work here at the ranch," Kaya said.

"I've got one, but she's on maternity leave." Flipping through a stack of folders in a file drawer, he removed one. "Here it is." He took an envelope from the folder.

Kaya wanted to hurl herself at Joshua, grab the envelope and run to her car, but she knew it wouldn't pay to reveal the full extent of her desperation. Remaining motionless, she waited and watched him read the document.

Looking inside the folder again, Joshua apparently saw something that turned his expression grim. The small scar above the left corner of his upper lip stood out pale against his tanned skin.

"Well, well. Look what else I found." Joshua held up a five-by-seven photograph so Kaya could see it. "Recognize him? Remember the man you deserted?"

A rush of pain and anxiety caused her heart to skip a beat and then resume beating doubly hard and fast. "Derrick," she whispered. Kaya pressed her hand against her chest to calm her heart's frantic rhythm. "I didn't desert him. It wasn't like that." Looking at the photo, she murmured, "Sometimes I forget how incredibly handsome he was."

"Yeah. Everybody around here called him the 'golden boy' from the time he could sit up."

Was there a slightly odd undertone in Joshua's deep voice? It had never occurred to Kaya that Joshua, being an ordinary-looking man, might resent the breathtaking handsomeness of his younger half brother. Except Kaya had never considered Joshua ordinary. He wasn't handsome by male-model standards, but he was rock-solid dependable and his own man who lived by a code of honor all his own. Even as the green young thing she had been when she had lived at the ranch, she had intuitively appreciated these qualities in Joshua. At times, disloyally, she had wished Derrick had inherited these traits rather than his heartbreaker looks.

And then there was something else about him that at

seventeen she had only sensed but hadn't been able to put a name to—an aura of pure maleness that contained more than a hint of raw sex appeal. Then as now, his male aura called to her on some primitive level, and then as now, it alarmed her and put her on her guard. Inexplicably the same danger that she sensed emanating from him, also hinted at dark, forbidden forces that sent a shiver of excitement through her blood stream.

Joshua started to put the photo back into the folder.

"Could I have it to g—" Kaya broke off, horrified. She had almost blurted out that she wanted to give the photo to her daughter. To Derrick's daughter. After being so vigilant all these years, she had almost blown it. Quickly she repeated, "Could I please have the photo?"

"Why? What did you do with yours? Tear them up to wipe out all traces of the man who adored you so much that your leaving killed him?"

Kaya felt as if Joshua had slammed his big fist into her chest, knocking the breath out of her body. "Is that what you think? That Derrick wrecked his car and killed himself because I left him?" she asked, her lips trembling. "Not even you can believe that. You can't!"

"Well, maybe you weren't there in person to make him take that curve at a hundred miles an hour, but you were there with him—up here." Joshua tapped his index finger against his temple. "And here," he said, placing his hand on his heart.

His eyes were merciless. Kaya shook her head. "No! You got it all wrong. He was drinking. You know he was. The newspaper article said so."

"And who drove him to the bottle?" Joshua asked, his voice unrelenting. "Who hammered at him day and night?

I couldn't understand the words through the walls, but I heard your voices. His voice pleading. What didn't you give him, Kaya? And your voice. Yours I heard all the time. Always at him. Now you have the gall to claim you didn't drive him to drink? How dumb do you think I am?"

Reeling from this new verbal blow, all Kaya could do was protest feebly. "It wasn't me. I didn't make him climb into a bottle. You don't know—"

"What don't I know? That when he couldn't lay a fortune at your feet fast enough to suit you, you left him to find someone who could? If you'd stayed with him just a little longer, you'd have gotten all the money you could ever want. If you'd stayed, he would be alive today."

Kaya wanted to protest this unjust and untrue accusation, but looking into Joshua's face, she realized she didn't have the time it would take to convince him of the truth. That is, if time alone could change his mind which at this moment she seriously doubted. Tears shot into her eyes. She tried to blink them away. Why did she mind so much what Joshua thought? It didn't matter. Nothing mattered but Natalie. The thought of her daughter launched her into action.

"Why don't you tell me what the document says? Do you enjoy torturing me?"

"Did you enjoy torturing my brother? You knew your leaving would cause Derrick pain."

"No more than the pain he caused me by letting me go."

They glared at each other. Finally Kaya said, "The document? What does it say? May I have the money?"

"Not so fast. I want my attorney to go over it. It has been a long time since this settlement was drawn up."

Appalled, Kaya realized that Joshua had decided to be

difficult. He was toying with her. Did he expect her to beg for the money? More to the point, would it do any good to beg? She didn't think so.

"I'll let you know as soon as I've talked to my lawyer. Where can I reach you?"

Alarm surged through Kaya. She couldn't give him her address. He might find out about Natalie. "I'll call you here at the ranch," she managed to say, her voice weak with defeat. She hated the sound of it. Suddenly anger, red-hot, boiling, rushed into every cell of her being.

Facing Joshua squarely, she said, "The amount of money in that account is little more than spending money to you, so why don't you give it to me and be done with it? Why are you playing this cruel game? Of all the Cunninghams, I thought you were the least heartless, but obviously I was mistaken. You've become every bit as hateful as Lily. Are you proud of that?"

Swiftly, like a rattlesnake striking, Joshua grabbed her arm. "I'm not the least like Lily," he ground out, "and you of all people should know that."

His blue eyes had turned dark, their expression hard. Kaya pulled her arm free of his hold. "I judge by what I see, and what I see is someone intent on petty revenge for real or imaginary hurts, and that was always Lily's specialty."

They stared at each other. Kaya didn't think she even blinked.

Joshua was the first to avert his gaze. He placed the folder into the file cabinet.

For a split second Kaya thought her legs would collapse. Suddenly she felt exhausted and at the end of her rope.

"I better leave," she murmured. Because she was fighting tears, Kaya didn't see the briefcase on the floor. Her foot caught on it, pitching her forward and straight into Joshua Cunningham's arms.

Chapter Two

Joshua rushed forward and caught Kaya.

His arms enfolded her. For an instant she rested against him. Kaya's scent, the clean smell of soap, of shampoo that reminded him of apple blossoms, filled his senses, causing a forgotten memory to rise from the dark recesses of his mind.

Once before, after a particularly ugly scene with Lily, he had caught her and held her when tears had caused her to stumble. Then as now, he had held her shapely body against his chest, his hand resting against her long, black hair. And then as now, a shiver of desire coursed through him. Odd, how this carefully repressed memory surfaced now.

"I'm sorry," Kaya said and took a step back. Her face flushed with embarrassment. "I broke my wrist in a fall not long ago, so now I usually look to see what's on the ground. I don't know how I could have missed seeing that briefcase. Thanks for catching me."

Joshua scowled. "Did you think I'd deliberately let you fall?"

"Well, if I'd broken my neck, your family would be rid of me once and for all. Rid of that ridiculously unsuitable wife Derrick inflicted on you."

Joshua swore softly. "You really think we're heartless through and through, don't you?"

Kaya shrugged. Joshua's hands still rested lightly against her waist. He seemed to be unaware of this and that was truly strange, because the Cunninghams weren't touchers, not even casual ones. She risked a quick look at his face. He looked thoughtful, preoccupied. That explained it, of course. Not that Joshua was incapable of touching a woman in passion, if the reputation he'd had in his younger years was anything to go by. "None of you gave me reason to think otherwise."

"Are you sure?" he demanded.

"Maybe your father did, but he was dying, so perhaps what I thought was kindness might have only been the exhaustion or the indifference caused by his illness."

Striving to sound casual, Joshua asked, "And me? You remember me as being only hateful to you?"

Kaya considered that for a second. "What I remember most about you, is the distance you kept. It was as if you couldn't stand to be in the same room with me. We rarely spent any time together, just you and me."

He murmured something that sounded like "with good reason," but Kaya couldn't be sure, for a clap of thunder obscured his voice. Kaya rubbed her wrist. "I knew it was going to rain," she said.

"That the one you broke?" Joshua asked, taking her left wrist into his hand.

"Yes."

"Still hurts?"

"Aches sometimes." She shifted her weight from one foot to the other foot.

So long ago, she'd instinctively thought of him as dangerous. Now he looked perfectly civilized and urbane in his expensive clothes, and yet all her senses warned her that he could be as lethal as any predator in nature.

"I've got to leave if I want to be home by midnight." She glanced pointedly at her hand which he still held.

Joshua didn't take the hint to release her hand. "How did you break your wrist?"

"My landlady's kids left a skateboard on the stairs."

"Did you sue for compensation?"

"No. She can hardly make ends meet as it is."

"Her homeowner's insurance would probably have covered it. Sounds to me like you're still as nice and naive as you were when you lived here."

"Not as naive. Nice? Maybe, though I realize the Cunninghams equate nice with dumb. Or worse."

"Not all Cunninghams," he corrected.

Kaya ignored his claim. "How soon will you contact your attorney about the account?"

Joshua's eyes narrowed. "You are desperate for that money, aren't you?"

Silently Kaya cursed herself for her carelessness. Hadn't she learned the hard way how people pounced on even a hint of desperation like buzzards on a road kill? The Cunninghams were no exception.

"Tell me why you need the money so desperately."

"I don't." Kaya wasn't sure her denial was convincing. "And even if I did, the reason isn't any of your business."

"Does it have to do with you breaking your wrist?"

Indirectly it did. She'd had to take time off from work, and since she was relatively new in the job, she didn't have enough sick days to cover her absence. Even a week without pay had made a big dent in her small savings account.

Then when Natalie had gotten ill and the insurance didn't cover all medical expenses, the remainder of her savings had been swallowed up alarmingly fast.

"I have to go. Please let go of my hand," she said. When he did, she left the room. Though she was aware that he was right behind her as she walked to the front door, she forced herself to keep a dignified pace.

When she opened the door, a guest of wind wrenched it from her hand. A flash of lightning zigzagged across the sky. It would rain long before she was anywhere near home.

"Well, goodbye, then," she said and ran toward her car. She knew Joshua watched her from the front porch.

Kaya started the car and blinked in disbelief when the engine warning sign flashed on. "Now what?" she muttered before she saw that the temperature gauge shot up into the danger zone. Could the radiator have sprung a leak? She shut the engine off and pulled the hood release.

"What's wrong?" Joshua asked.

"I don't know. Seems the car's overheating."

Joshua popped the hood and examined the radiator. "Looks like one of the hoses is leaking."

"Oh great. How far is the nearest service station?" Kaya asked.

"Let me get Mike. He's the ranch mechanic."

Kaya stared at her car's engine with a frown. Why did this have to happen now? Still, if it had to happen, it was better to have car trouble at the ranch than on a deserted stretch of the highway. She sighed.

"I hope I didn't interrupt your dinner," Kaya said when Joshua came back with a man he introduced as Mike.

"Nah, just kept me from eating another piece of pie

which I don't need," Mike said, patting his stomach. "Let's see what we got here."

Kaya stepped back to let him examine the engine.

"Busted radiator hose," he announced.

Kaya sighed. "You wouldn't happen to have a spare one lying around?"

"None that would fit your compact. I can get you one in the morning."

"In the morning?"

"I'm sorry, but that's the best I can do. Good night," Mike said and walked off.

"Thank you," Kaya called after him. Turning to Joshua, she said, her voice anguished, "But I have to get home tonight."

"We can't get a replacement until tomorrow, and you can't drive with a busted hose. Looks like you'll have to spend the night whether you like it or not." Joshua placed his hand on her elbow and urged her toward the house.

When they reached the porch, a crash of thunder made Kaya jump. "I hate to impose on your hospitality," she said as they entered the house.

"You're not imposing. Besides, we're going to have a hell of a storm. I wouldn't turn a dog out in weather like this."

"Then you put me in good company. I like dogs."

Joshua snapped his fingers. "I remember you befriending that half-starved puppy that showed up one day."

"I could identify with him. We had a lot in common. We both lacked a fine pedigree and were about as welcome on the Diamond C as an outbreak of anthrax."

"You gave him some grand-sounding name. What was it?"

"Duke. He had so little going for him, I thought he deserved a grand name."

"I've always wondered about your name, Kaya. It's unusual."

"I was named after my Indian grandmother." Thinking of the dog, Kaya sighed. "One day Duke disappeared. You helped me look for him."

His voice gentle, Joshua said, "He was a stray, used to roaming."

Kaya shook her head. "No. He'd found a home and someone to love him. He wouldn't have left voluntarily."

Joshua pounced on her statement. "You did. You'd found a home and someone to love you, and you left."

St. Peter reading her sins from the big book at heaven's gate couldn't sound more condemning than Joshua.

"Well? Nothing to say in your defense?"

Was Joshua trying to provoke her into an argument with him? Well, she wouldn't let him. In the morning she intended to leave the ranch with as much of her pride and her dignity intact as she could manage. "You're wrong, just as wrong as I had been. I thought I had found love and a home, but I hadn't. And if you insist on dissecting the past, I'm going out that front door, rain or no rain, and wait for morning on the porch."

Joshua lifted his hands in a mollifying gesture. "Okay, okay. Why don't we see what Clancy cooked for dinner? I'm starving." When he saw her hesitate, he added, "I'm positive there's enough food. Clancy never heard of nouvelle cuisine. He still identifies comfort with a table loaded with food."

From where she stood, Kaya could see into the formal dining room, the scene of her many subtle and not so subtle humiliations at the hands of Lily who loved to cut up the people present the way she cut her steak—with the skill of a professional butcher. Most often, her primary target had been Kaya. She hated that coldly elegant room. Shivering, she hugged her arms around her waist.

"Are you coming down with something?" Joshua asked.

"No." That would be the last straw. She couldn't afford to get sick.

"What's wrong?"

"Nothing. Can we eat in the kitchen, please?"

"Sure, why not? I don't think the dining room's been used more than three or four times since Lily left. I like eating in the kitchen myself." Joshua placed his hand lightly against Kaya's back, urging her forward.

His touch made her nerve endings twitch and quiver. She wanted nothing more than to run, to escape, but that would have revealed her weakness. She knew better than to do that.

In the kitchen, Joshua took two covered pots from the oven. Lifting the lid of one, he sniffed. "Mmm. Diamond C beef strips in mushroom sauce." Lifting the other lid, he announced, "And potatoes and carrots. Clancy usually makes a salad that he leaves in the refrigerator. We can divide that between us. He doesn't eat rabbit food, as he calls it. And apple pie with vanilla ice cream for dessert. Does that sound good to you?"

"It sounds delicious."

The meal tasted heavenly, she discovered. Since Natalie had gotten ill, Kaya hadn't eaten anything except cereal and milk or a hastily fixed sandwich with an occasional apple or orange thrown in. She had almost forgotten what a satisfying experience a good meal was.

Only when she had sated her fiercest hunger did Kaya wonder why Joshua had invited her to share his meal. From his earlier comments she knew he blamed her for the breakup of her marriage to his half brother and for Derrick's subsequent death. So what was Joshua up to? Why was he being nice to her? What did he want? Whatever it was, and she was certain he had an ulterior motive, she'd better be on guard. She sat up straighter.

When Joshua brought the pie and the ice cream to the table and served each of them, he said, "There's something I've always wondered about. Why did you refuse an annulment and insist on a divorce?"

He had asked the question in such a conversational tone that she had almost blurted out the truth: she had wanted her child to be legitimate, to be entitled to her father's name without anybody raising an eyebrow. True, when the attorney had approached her with the annulment she hadn't known that she was pregnant. She should have known, but she had been so unhappy that she paid little attention to her body. Perhaps subconsciously she had been aware that she was carrying a new life, and perhaps that had made her refuse the annulment.

"An annulment would have been an out-and-out lie. Like saying Derrick and I had never been married. Though Lily tried hard to pretend that we weren't husband and wife, we were."

Joshua nodded. "I remember the night Derrick brought you home and introduced you as his wife. Lily, after throwing a major temper tantrum, put you in the guest room and fully expected Derrick to spend the night in the room he'd occupied since he was a baby. She was not happy when the golden boy didn't fall in with her plan." Joshua chuckled at the memory.

"If I'd been older and more experienced, I would have

recognized that incident as Lily's declaration of war. But I wasn't. I thought maybe separate bedrooms were a custom in the houses of the rich and the socially prominent. Lily and your father had separate bedrooms."

"They didn't when they were first married," Joshua said.

"I bet as soon as she got everything she wanted, she found some excuse to get a room for herself. She always struck me as a cold woman," Kaya said.

"Snoring."

"Pardon?"

"Lily claimed my father's snoring kept her awake." Joshua let his gaze drift over Kaya in an assessing manner. "I bet you're not a cold woman."

Joshua's velvety voice almost purred those words. They fell on her ears like a warm caress. In the dark, that voice would be like liquid heat, murmuring wicked, roguish suggestions and sweet little lies. His voice went a long way toward explaining why Joshua never lacked for female attention. Why was she even thinking about Joshua Cunningham's bedroom voice? The man had no use for her, and she had reason to fear and distrust him.

"Why are you being nice to me, Joshua?"

He reached across the table to touch her hand. "Relax."

That was easy for him to say. How could she relax, with him rubbing his thumb over the back of her hand? What kind of gesture was that anyway? A seductive one, she answered herself, when she felt her breathing change. That would never do. With deliberate precision she used her free hand to lift his hand off the one he had captured.

"Could I have more coffee, please?" she asked. Not that she needed any more. She was already wired and running high on caffeine, but it was a good way to get Joshua's attention focused on something else. She noticed that Joshua's lips twitched with amusement, as if recognizing her tactic.

"More coffee coming up," he said.

"I'll get it," Kaya said, jumping up. She refilled their cups. When she returned the pot to the counter, she looked out the kitchen window. The storm raged outside.

"You're not afraid of a little thunder and lightning are you?"

"No, though there's nothing little about this storm." Kaya came back to the table and sat down.

"Then what is it?"

She shrugged. "Maybe being back in this house. Reliving all those memories." When she saw Joshua's expression harden, she knew he was remembering all the things he held against her. She was not up to more recriminations. Quickly she changed the subject.

"Speaking of this house. Now that it's yours, aren't you going to remarry? It's the kind of house that should have children in it to give it some warmth."

"How did you know I got married?"

"Your marriage announcement was in the newspaper."

"How do you know I haven't remarried?" he asked.

"The same way I knew you had gotten married. The newspapers." Kaya watched him quietly over the rim of her cup. "Why aren't you married? You're surely old enough."

"I'm thirty-four. That's hardly over the hill," Joshua said. "I'll get around to it again one of these days." He drained his cup. Then looking at Kaya challengingly, he demanded, "Why haven't you remarried? Surely a woman as pretty as you has had offers."

"How do you know I haven't remarried?"

"No rings. You're traditional enough that you'd wear a wedding band."

"If you aren't over the hill, then I certainly am not either. I might get around to it."

The corners of Joshua's mouth twitched, fighting a smile. "For a small woman, you sure are sassy. In a soft-spoken sort of way. That got to Lily more than if you'd lowered yourself to yelling and name-calling which was her natural style. You always came off a lot more ladylike than she did. That surely galled her."

"I didn't know I got to her," Kaya said, surprised. "She scared the living daylights out of me. She was everything I was not: tall, worldly, dressed and groomed as if she'd stepped from the pages of a fashion magazine. She looked like she came from generations of money and privilege."

Joshua laughed. "Lily liked to pretend that she did. The truth is, she grew up on a little scrub farm where they raised more kids than anything else. She was shrewd, though. And determined. I'll give her that."

"Tell me about her."

"She came to Abilene, looked and watched and learned. She started in a hamburger joint and worked her way up to being hostess in an executive club where most of the influential businessmen ate. It was the best hunting ground for rich men, so it was no accident that she got a job there. When my dad met her, my mom had been gone for a few years. He was lonely and vulnerable. No match for a man trap like Lilybelle."

"Lilybelle? Is that really her name? I never knew." Kaya tried valiantly to suppress a smile.

"It's one of the best-kept secrets in the state of Texas. I didn't know it until I came across some documents after my father's death. She hates that name. Thinks it sounds old-fashioned and countrified. If she ever finds out I told you, she'll come after me with a shotgun."

"Since I'm not ever planning to meet her again, your secret's safe with me." Kaya stared thoughtfully at the table. "I didn't know about her background. You'd think that since she grew up poor like me, she would have been more accepting."

"I suspect you reminded her too much of a time in her life she'd sooner forget. She liked to pretend that she'd always had wealth and position. She never let any of her relatives come to the Diamond C, not even when she got married. She sent them money but kept them away."

"And then her son married a girl who came from a family that was just as poor. No wonder she hated me."

"If it's any comfort, Lily would have disliked any girl Derrick married."

"Probably," Kaya conceded.

Both Kaya and Joshua looked toward the door as the curtains on the window whipped in the breeze from the opening back door. A moment later Clancy burst into the kitchen.

"Dang. That's some storm. Thought it would blow me clean into the next county." He removed his hat and the rain poncho he'd worn.

"Why didn't you stay in the bunkhouse till the rain let up?" Joshua asked.

"Thought you folks might need some help with supper."

"We helped ourselves. Have you eaten?" Joshua asked.

"Ate a few bites at the bunkhouse but honestly this storm has me off my feed."

"Does it look like the storm's letting up?" Kaya asked.

"No. Looks worse. I think we're in for it till midnight

or later," Clancy said. "I better get a room ready for you, Miss Kaya."

"Clancy, I can put clean sheets on a bed. You've had a long day."

"The front corner room and the room next to the sleepin' porch were cleaned two days ago," Clancy said.

"She'll take the porch room," Joshua said.

It took Kaya a second to realize that the front room Clancy had mentioned was the room she had occupied during her marriage. "The porch room will be fine," she said, sending Joshua a grateful look.

Clancy removed the red bandana he wore around his neck and mopped his forehead. "Is it hot in here?"

"Not particularly." Kaya looked at Clancy closely. His face was flushed and his eyes looked feverish. "How do you feel?" she asked, walking toward him.

"Not so good," he admitted reluctantly.

"You look like you have a fever." Kaya laid a practiced hand on Clancy's forehead. "You feel hot to me."

"I'm okay. I'll clean up down here and show you to your room, then I'll lie down."

"I can find the room by myself, and I'll wash up. You go and lie down. Maybe we should take your temperature first," Kaya suggested.

"Nah, I'll be okay. A good night's sleep, and I'll be as right as rain." Clancy walked toward the door. "Good night, y'all."

When they heard him mount the stairs, Joshua said, "It's not like Clancy to give in so easy. He must really feel sick. Maybe I should call Doc Wiggins."

"Why don't you look in on Clancy when you go up. The doctor would have a hard time getting here in this storm. If Clancy isn't better by morning, you can call him then."

With that said Kaya got up and began to clear the table.

"Can I help?" Joshua asked.

"With the dishes?"

"Well, yes."

The image that flashed through Kaya's mind made her grin.

"What's so funny?" he asked, intrigued.

"I had a vision."

"Of what?"

"You," she said gravely, while valiantly trying to suppress a chuckle. She didn't succeed. "A vision of you wearing a little white apron with ruffles."

Joshua looked at her with a raised eyebrow. "That's all it ever will be...a vision."

"Too bad. You looked real cute," Kaya said with an almost straight face.

Joshua braced his hands against his waist, fighting the grin that tugged at his mouth. "Cute? You call a cowboy cute? You should be banned from the State of Texas." Joshua had tried to sound stern but knew he failed. He liked it when Kaya relaxed enough to tease him. "A white-faced calf is cute. Or a puppy. Not somebody my size."

He was right, of course. He was a force of nature—strong, dominant, sexy. Sexy? How had that word sneaked into her mind? Quickly Kaya redirected her thoughts.

Joshua was watching her. Kaya could feel his gaze. She remained silent as long as she could. "Why don't you just ask me what you're dying to know?"

"I'm curious. What have you been doing since you left the Diamond C?" It was an innocent question, but he saw Kaya's back stiffen. She stayed turned away from him.

"I finished high school. Then I worked."

"What kind of work did you do?"

She tossed the dish towel on the counter and faced him, her green eyes flashing. "Any job that I could get that was honest. Work where I paid income tax and social security and all the rest of it—"

"Hold on. You're jumping to conclusions again. I didn't imply that you did anything dishonest."

Kaya realized she'd been wrong. "No, I guess you didn't, but your stepmother certainly did. When I wanted Derrick to leave the ranch with me and both of us get jobs, she taunted me, saying that the only way I could earn money was on my back!"

Joshua's brows drew together in a fierce scowl. "That woman has a tongue like a viper and a mind like an open sewer. I know you've worked hard."

Kaya crossed her arms over her chest. "And how do you know that?"

"From your hands."

Kaya raised her hands to look at them. Frowning, she said, "I don't understand."

"If you hadn't done hard work, you'd have pampered hands with those long, fake, glued on fingernails. Come to think of it, Lily has nails like that."

"I always thought they looked like claws, dripping with fresh blood," Kaya murmured. Realizing she'd said that loud enough for Joshua to hear, she added, "I'm sorry. She *is* your stepmother and helped raise you."

Joshua shook his head. "Clancy was probably more of a mother to me than Lily. Let's not talk about her. Tell me about you."

Kaya realized Joshua wasn't about to quit asking questions until she gave him a few answers. "I live in Abilene and work for a delivery service." She folded the dish towel. "Joshua, I'm tired. May I go up to the porch room now?"

"Sure, come with me."

They walked side by side. Joshua was aware of her every step of the way. When her arm accidentally brushed against his, he felt as if he'd been zapped with an electric cattle prod.

When they passed the room she had shared with her husband, Kaya's steps faltered for a beat. Then her pace increased as if she couldn't get away fast enough.

"Here we are," Joshua said and switched on the reading lamp behind the upholstered chair. "The bathroom's next door. You should find a new toothbrush in one of the drawers and everything else you need. I'll see if I can find something you can sleep in. I'll be right back."

Left alone, Kaya looked at the room. She didn't remember it looking like this, so Lily must have had it redecorated. As it adjoined the sleeping porch the family used before air-conditioning was added, the room continued the wicker and flowered chintz motif of the porch. Lily had probably used the interior decorating firm that redid the entire house from time to time. They had done an outstanding job. Kaya sighed. What she wouldn't give if she could offer Natalie a bedroom like this of her own.

Joshua returned. "This T-shirt is the best I can do."

Kaya accepted it. "Thank you. It'll be fine. Good night."

After she showered and brushed her teeth, she donned the T-shirt. It was big enough to cover her decently. In the room she discovered a telephone. She picked up the phone and then put it down. As desperately as she wanted to talk to Natalie, she couldn't take the risk. She knew she didn't have enough minutes left on her phone card for a long distance call, and it was unlikely that the hospital would accept a collect call. Joshua would probably notice and question a call made from his house to an Abilene hospital. As curious as he was about her, he might trace the call and find out about Natalie. She wouldn't risk that.

Though she was certain that after the tension of the day she would have a hard time falling asleep, she went out like a light.

She awoke a few minutes after eight o'clock. She couldn't believe she'd slept that late. Still, it was unlikely that the new radiator hose had arrived at the ranch already. She washed her face and brushed her teeth. In the hall she met Clancy who looked very sick.

"Clancy, where do you think you're going?"

"Gotta fix a pot of coffee for Josh."

"You'll do no such thing. Get back into bed. You look awful. I'm taking your temperature," she announced in a voice that always got results with her daughter. It also worked with Clancy. He stumbled back into bed. Kaya fetched the thermometer she'd seen in the medicine cabinet and took his temperature.

Joshua joined them.

"You better call the doctor," she told him. "Clancy's temperature is almost a hundred and three."

While Joshua phoned the doctor, Kaya went to the kitchen and brought a glass of juice and a pitcher of cold water to put on Clancy's bedside table. Clancy downed the juice thirstily.

Back in the kitchen she brewed a pot of coffee.

"Mike fixed your car. And Doc Wiggins will be here at noon. Can you stay till he gets here?" Joshua asked.

Kaya shook her head. "I'd like to, but I have a prior commitment I have to keep."

"Some hot date with a special guy?" Joshua asked rather nastily. "That's more important than Clancy who always treated you decently?"

Silently Kaya counted to five before she answered. "It's not a date with a guy, but I have to keep this appointment. I'm sorry."

"Yeah, right."

"There you go again, assuming the worst about me. Why do you always do that? If my appointment weren't truly important, don't you think I'd stay?" Joshua looked at her with those blue Cunningham eyes that had turned hard, making Kaya feel even worse about leaving Clancy than she already did.

"I have no idea what you'd do. All I know from past experience is that you leave when the going gets tough."

She clenched her hands into fists and ground her teeth until they hurt, but she managed to control her temper. She needed Joshua's goodwill. Natalie's welfare depended on it—Natalie who was waiting for her at the hospital. Whose head might be pounding with pain, who… Kaya had to stop anticipating trouble.

Looking at Joshua pleadingly, she said, "Please believe that if I could, I'd stay." His expression remained cold. She might as well plead for understanding from a stone statue. "I'm sorry, but I have to go." She hurried out of the house.

Joshua followed her. Watching her small car drive away, he memorized her license plate number.

Chapter Three

Kaya lifted her arm to wipe her forehead on the sleeve of her blouse. It was a warm, humid day, but she was perspiring out of all proportion to the temperature in the shipping room. She also had a headache. The four extra strength headache pills she had taken hadn't even dulled the pain.

The throbbing ache extended all the way down to the area behind her eyes. As she hefted a sixty-pound box onto the conveyor belt, the muscles in her arms and shoulders ached. She hurt all over. Glancing at the clock, she saw that she still had thirty minutes to go before quitting time. She wasn't sure she could make it.

She did, but just. By the time she had climbed the stairs to her apartment, her legs and arms trembled from the effort. She stuck the thermometer under her tongue. While waiting for it to measure her temperature, she curled up on the couch.

When she became aware of her surroundings again, thirty minutes had passed. She must have dozed off, with the thermometer still in her mouth. Her temperature had shot up to the hundred and two mark. Kaya groaned. That meant she probably wouldn't be able to visit Natalie.

When she phoned the hospital, the head nurse of pediatrics confirmed her suspicion. She wouldn't be allowed on the ward until she had been fever free for twenty-four hours. The nurse was kind enough to transfer Kaya's call to Natalie's room.

"Hi, sweetie. How are you today?" Kaya asked, making her voice chipper.

"Okay. Aren't you coming to see me tonight, Mommy?"

"I can't. Looks like I've caught some nasty flu bug, so they won't let me in until I've licked it."

"Like the time you had a cold and sore throat?"

"Yeah. But don't worry. I'm going to drink gallons of orange juice and herb tea with honey and lemon, and by the weekend I should be able to come. I'll bring you a surprise."

"What?" Natalie asked eagerly. "A new book from the library?"

"If I tell you, it wouldn't be a surprise, would it?"

"No," Natalie agreed reluctantly.

"You be a good girl and eat all your supper. Promise?"

"I promise, Mommy."

"And don't forget to say your prayers."

"I won't. I'll say a prayer for you, too."

A lump formed in Kaya's throat. "I love you, sweetie. Sleep tight." She replaced the receiver. Then she picked it up again. She started to dial her cousin's number when she remembered that Maria was out of town.

All Kaya wanted to do was curl up on the couch and sleep. But since she had promised Natalie she would lick this bug quickly, she dragged herself to the kitchen for a big glass of juice. While she drank it, she glanced at the mail. The bill she had been expecting, the bill she couldn't pay unless Joshua came through with the money, lay on top. She would wait two more days before she called Joshua. She didn't look forward to that call, but she had to make it.

The next morning Kaya's temperature had dropped down to a hundred. She felt marginally better, but with the unpaid medical bills looming, she had to go to work.

By noon she thought she would pass out. The idea of food repelled her. She decided to spend her lunch break lying down in the back seat of her car.

The parking lot swayed like the deck of a ship. She would have fallen if someone hadn't reached out to steady her.

"What's the matter with you, Kaya?"

The voice was pleasant, and it was familiar, but she felt too dizzy to concentrate on it. She kept her gaze on the ground, trying to make it stop swaying. A cool hand touched her forehead.

"You're burning up with fever. Looks like you've caught Clancy's flu."

She lifted her gaze. "Joshua? How did you find me?"

"You told me you worked for a delivery service, so it wasn't all that hard. Where do you live?"

"Why?"

"So I can take you home. You belong in bed."

"I can get myself home."

"I doubt that you can make it across this parking lot by yourself."

"I'll be okay," she insisted.

"Is somebody at your place who can take care of you?"

"No, but I can take care of myself."

"Yeah, right," Joshua muttered. Still holding her up, he made a quick decision. With gentle force, he moved her toward his car. "Doesn't matter where you live because I couldn't stay in town long enough to take care of you."

Kaya made a feeble attempt to resist when Joshua put her into the front seat and fastened her seat belt. The moment she sat down, her eyes drooped shut. "Where are we going?"

"To the ranch."

"No! I can't go there. I can't leave work just like this," she protested.

"I'll call your boss and explain."

Kaya tried to object vigorously. She even attempted to get out of the car, but her body was too weak to obey her will. Maybe after she had rested for a few minutes she would be able to get out at the next red traffic light. Yes, that's what she would do, she decided, drifting into a fevered sleep.

Kaya opened her eyes and saw delicate floral garlands on a pale blue background. When had she changed the wallpaper in her bedroom? She had been meaning to do it since the day she had moved into the apartment. Finally she had gotten around to it, she thought, pleased and closed her eyes again.

"Kaya, drink this."

That lovely male voice again. It was soothing. As soothing and comforting as the strong hand which moved her hot, heavy hair off her face. The hand slid behind her neck to raise her head. When the edge of a glass touched her lips, Kaya drank the sweet-tart, cold liquid it contained.

Opening her eyes, she saw him. "Joshua? What are you doing here?"

"Taking care of you."

"You can't be here. I must be dreaming."

"That's right. You're dreaming. Now hush and go back to your dream."

A dream. Of course, it was a dream, but what a dream! Joshua Cunningham, the sexy, larger-than-life Diamond C boss was gently, ever so gently, wiping her face with a cool, damp washcloth. And her neck. And all the way down between her breasts where she was wet with perspiration. He had magic hands. And a magic voice. With a small sigh she slid back into the dark sleep that reached out to claim her.

The next time she escaped from the fevered dreams, she escaped completely and instantly. She knew immediately where she was: in the porch room at the ranch. She didn't remember how she got there. She didn't know how long ago that had been.

Natalie! How worried she must be, not having heard from her mother for…oh God. If only she knew how long she had been at the ranch. The clock on the nightstand told her that it was midmorning, but of what day?

Kaya swung her legs over the side of the bed. The room didn't sway, but she knew she was so weak that she wouldn't get very far. There was a telephone, she remembered. Locating it with her eyes, she inched her way toward it. She would have to chance a call.

Praying that nobody would come in while she was on the phone, she picked up the receiver. By the time she got through to the hospital, she was shaking with exhaustion.

"Sister Margaret? This is Kaya Cunningham."

"Thank heaven, you called."

"What's wrong with Natalie? What happened?" Kaya asked, her heart firmly lodged in her throat.

"Natalie's okay. Don't panic and imagine the worst case scenario."

"I'm sorry," Kaya murmured. "I know I do that. Jump to conclusions and imagine the worst."

"Yes, you do," Sister Margaret said. "Anyway, when you didn't call for two days, I got worried. I phoned your place of work. Your boss told me you were out sick. I called your apartment. When there was no answer I asked your landlady to go up and check on you. I was afraid you might be delirious with fever."

"I've been floating in and out of consciousness for...did you say two days?"

"Yes."

"Oh, my God! Natalie must be so worried, not hearing from me all that time."

"We managed to keep her calm. And you know her. She can hide her pain and her feelings amazingly well. She clings to your promise that you'll come this weekend."

"I'll be there if I have to crawl the whole way."

"Don't you dare. You know that with her kind of condition it's important that she not be exposed to any infectious diseases."

"I know. I won't come until I've beaten this fever."

"I do have a bone to pick with you, Kaya. You know how vital it is for us to be able to reach you."

"I know, and I'm sorry I was out of touch. I called as soon as I was physically able."

"Where are you?"

Kaya knew she had no choice but to tell Sister Margaret where she was. "Will you promise to call here only in an emergency?"

"Of course."

"If you call, promise you won't mention that you're from a hospital and above all, please, please, don't mention Natalie. Please just say that you're a friend of mine and need to talk to me."

"I am your friend, but why this secrecy about Natalie?"

"Because I don't want to risk losing custody of my daughter! I can't! Please—"

"Calm down, Kaya. There's no reason for you to be this upset. I'll do what you ask of me, provided…are you listening?"

"Yes." Kaya repressed her sobs. "I'm listening."

"I'll do as you asked if you go back to bed right now and rest."

"I will. Can I speak to Natalie?"

"First give me the phone number where I can reach you."

Kaya did.

"You can talk for three minutes. Both of you need rest."

A woman of her word, Sister Margaret took the phone from Natalie in exactly three minutes. That was just as well, as Kaya heard footsteps in the hall. With strength born of desperation, she lunged for the bed and dove under the sheet. The effort left her breathless and trembling. She closed her eyes, pretending to be asleep.

Moments later the now familiar hand rested against her forehead, checking her fever. His scent, a mixture of leather, of horses, of the outdoors, of soap aromatic with a blend of pine and woodsy ferns, was now familiar, too.

"Finally," she heard the warm voice murmur. He seemed relieved. When his fingers trailed over her cheek to seek the pulse point at the side of her throat, she opened her eyes, alarmed. Her pulse was probably still fast from her mad dash to the bed.

"It wasn't a dream after all," she said to distract him. It worked. Joshua's fingers jerked from her throat.

"Your fever broke during the night."

"How do you know that?" When he didn't reply and the answer dawned on her, Kaya was momentarily speechless. Finally she said, "You sat up with me, didn't you?"

"Last time I checked, that wasn't a crime," Joshua said, his tone defensive.

"I'm sorry. I didn't mean to sound ungrateful, but you shouldn't have. Just as you shouldn't have brought me here. I'm not your responsibility."

"Oh, I don't know about that. You caught the flu in this house."

When Kaya tried to sit up, Joshua placed two fingers on her chin. This slight pressure was sufficient to keep her down. She was that weak.

"Stay put. I'll send Clancy up with some food. You need to regain your strength."

Kaya could do nothing but watch Joshua walk out of the room. As much as she hated to admit it, he was right. She felt worn out. The few steps she'd taken to make the phone call had exhausted her. If she wanted to be ready to visit Natalie by the weekend, she had to recoup her strength.

The sound of Clancy setting the tray on the nightstand, woke her. Kaya couldn't believe she had fallen asleep again in the short interval between Joshua's leaving and Clancy's arrival. But she had.

"Brought you something to eat, Miss Kaya. Dry toast, tea, and orange juice. It ain't much. I'll fix you somethin' more solid for lunch, if you can keep this down."

Kaya sat up. "Thank you, Clancy. How are you?"

"Just fine now." He placed the tray over her lap and urged her to eat.

She must have been famished for the two slices of dry toast tasted delicious.

"You sure was sick, Miss Kaya. When Josh carried you into the house, you was out of your mind with fever. I guess you caught the flu from me. I'm sure sorry about that."

"It's not your fault. Besides, you helped take care of me."

"Some. Josh did most of the sittin' up with you. I said it weren't necessary because you slept most of the time, but he did anyway. You know how bullheaded he is."

Clancy went on to talk about events at the ranch, but Kaya listened only halfheartedly as she pondered Clancy's astonishing revelations. Joshua, who harbored a deep bitterness toward her, had sacrificed his sleep to sit up with her. That made no sense, she thought, finishing her tea. But then bringing her to the Diamond C made no sense either. The man was an enigma.

"I'll leave the juice on the nightstand. You can finish it later. You need to rest now," Clancy said, taking the tray.

"Thank you, Clancy."

"You're welcome. If you need anything, just holler. I'll leave the door open so I can hear you."

Kaya slid into a lying position. Odd, how something as simple as eating tired her out. In the silence of the lovely room, disjointed images flitted through her mind. Images of Joshua. Of him bending over her, murmuring quieting words. Of him urging her to take medicine. Of him brushing something from her bare legs.

As hard as she tried, she couldn't remember anything more explicit. It was only a flicker of a memory, as unstable and insubstantial as an elusive melody heard long ago.

Still, the memory troubled her, especially the bare legs. How had she come to be undressed, wearing only her panties and one of Joshua's long T-shirts? Thinking of the possibilities, she could feel herself blush.

Joshua didn't come to her room until after dinner. When she saw him eyeing the T-shirt she wore, she felt obliged to explain.

"I asked Clancy for a clean T-shirt. I felt so sweaty and my hair was so matted and tangled that I had to take a shower. I hope you don't mind about the T-shirt."

"Looks a lot better on you than on me."

"Joshua, I keep remembering you brushing something from my legs. It's not a clear memory, but it is unpleasant."

"When you were delirious, you kept screaming that spiders were crawling up your legs. I couldn't get you quiet until I pretended to brush them off."

That explained the only vivid part of the memory: his strong fingers moving from her ankles to her knees to her thighs. The recollection of his touch swept color into her cheeks.

"Why couldn't I imagine satin sheets on my legs?"

Joshua's mouth eased into a small grin. "Are you afraid of spiders?"

She shrugged. "They're definitely not my favorite insects." Kaya considered how to phrase the question that had been troubling her since that morning.

"Why don't you just spit out what's bothering you," Joshua suggested after watching her silent struggle.

"I don't remember taking my clothes off," she blurted out, her eyes carefully avoiding his.

"You didn't take them off."

A small sound of dismay involuntarily escaped her throat. "I was afraid of that. Did you?" she prompted.

"Uh-huh."

Kaya groaned again.

"I had no choice. I couldn't leave you in those hot, tight jeans, not when you were burning up with fever, and the only other person here was Clancy. I couldn't ask him. He would have been too embarrassed. Anyway, I didn't take all your clothes off."

"You didn't leave many on either," she pointed out, remembering her panties.

"I put the T-shirt on you before I took your bra off."

"That takes considerable skill and practice," Kaya said, slanting him a telling look.

Joshua grinned. "What can I say? I'm no saint. I've had some experience with women."

"Oh, such modesty! Excuse me while I gag."

"You must be feeling better. Your sassy mouth is back."

"Yes, I'm feeling better. I should be able to go home tomorrow."

"What's your rush? The weekend's almost here. You don't work on Saturday, so you may as well stay here."

"Did you call my boss?"

"Yes. He said for you not to worry about the job and to get well. From the way he talked, you must be a good employee."

The approval in Joshua's eyes and voice made her feel warm all over. "About staying for the weekend, I'll wait and see how I feel," Kaya said. She couldn't stay the weekend, but this was no time to argue with Joshua. "Have you talked to your attorney yet?"

"No. I haven't had a chance, what with you getting sick and all."

Don't push, Kaya told herself. Reaching for the water pitcher, she emptied its contents into her glass and drank thirstily.

"Let me fill this up for you." Joshua carried the pitcher into the bathroom.

"I can do that," she called after him, but he'd already entered the bathroom. Drat. She had hung her panties and bra over the shower rod to dry. By his own admission, Joshua wasn't unacquainted with female lingerie, but it was still embarrassing.

When he returned, she flicked a quick glance at his face but his expression was unreadable.

"Here's your water," he said, setting the silver pitcher on the nightstand.

"Thanks."

Joshua turned toward the door.

"Joshua wait. I want to talk—"

"Later," he said and hurried out.

She had thought this would be a good time to discuss that account with him, pin him down on a specific date, extract a definite promise from him. What if Joshua refused to release those funds to her? Kaya shuddered. He was her last hope.

Though Kaya tried to maintain her optimism by telling herself that somehow she would get through this crisis as she had through all the others, her money worries followed her into her sleep. She dreamed that Natalie had been transferred to a different hospital, a hospital set high on a hill. Kaya could see the building clearly, but could not get to it. Every street became a maze filled with unnamable terrors lurking in shadowy doorways. Hands snatched at her, voices mocked her, pounding noises pursued her, giant spiders wove webs to block her path.

She woke up with a cry of fear. Her body jerked into a defensive crouching position. When she saw the lovely, sunlit room, she closed her eyes with a whimper of relief. A dream.

When she heard pounding noises, she dashed to the window in time to see half a dozen cowboys ride into the yard. Joshua was among them. What if he came upstairs to see her? This could be her last chance to talk to him about the money. Her hands flew to her tangled hair. What a mess. She ran to the bathroom to make herself as presentable as she could, with only a toothbrush, comb and a bar of soap as her tools.

No sooner had Kaya come out of the bathroom when she heard Clancy's voice yell up the stairs that she was wanted on the phone. It could only be Sister Margaret, and that meant an emergency. With shaking hands she picked up the receiver.

"This is Kaya Cunningham."

"Hello, Ms. Cunningham. This is Dr. Reiger."

Natalie's doctor. Blood rushed to Kaya's head and roared in her ears. "What's happened to Natalie?"

"Nothing. I'm sorry. I didn't mean to scare you. Actually I have good news. Remember the new treatment for Natalie's anemia I mentioned to you?"

"Yes."

"Well, the medication arrived. I'd like to start it today. Let me remind you of what I said earlier. It might not work with Natalie," he cautioned. "It doesn't with all patients, but it's worth a try. I need your consent, though."

"This is the drug that's very expensive, right?"

"Yes, but I'm quite sure we can get it at a reduced price. Maybe even for free since I'll offer to write an article about the drug for the medical journals."

"That would be wonderful, Dr. Reiger," Kaya said, her voice filled with warmth and gratitude. "I'll sign whatever forms are necessary."

"Is that a yes?"

"Go ahead. I'll do anything it takes. You know that."

"I was hoping you'd say that. I'll start the treatment today."

After saying goodbye, Kaya hung up with new hope in her heart. She whirled around when she heard a noise that sounded suspiciously like a derisive male snort. Joshua stood in the doorway, glowering at her.

"'I'll do anything it takes'?" He parodied her words in a sarcastic tone.

"Since when do Cunninghams eavesdrop on their guests?"

Joshua moved toward her with that slightly swaggering stride typical of men wearing cowboy boots. The aura of vitality and power he exuded made that stride both more appealing and more daunting. Instinctively Kaya backed up a couple of steps. Looking into his blue eyes made even bluer by a hot, dangerous gleam, she might have moved back even farther, but the dresser blocked her. Adrenaline poured into her bloodstream.

"It's not what you think," she said, watching him quickly close the distance between. She was trapped, but the primary emotion that coursed through her wasn't fear but excitement. It made no sense.

"And how do you know what I think?" he asked, his voice deceptively soft.

Joshua stopped so close to Kaya that she was forced to raise her head to look at him. The expression on his face paralyzed her vocal chords.

Wrapping her long, luxurious hair around his fingers, Joshua gently urged her even closer against him. "Do you know what it does to a man to hear you promise to do anything for him in that sincere, hot, husky tone?"

Held captive by his gaze, unable to move or speak, Kaya watched Joshua's face lean closer and closer. He was going to kiss her. Joshua Cunningham was going to kiss her. Bewildered and thrilled, she felt waves of heat thrum through her body. She held his searing gaze until it threatened to consume her. Her eyelids drifted shut. Her lips parted slightly.

Why had she ever thought his mouth thin and cruel? It wasn't. Slanted over hers, his lips wooed her expertly, eliciting a response she certainly hadn't ever wanted to give again to any man. Even as her brain reminded her of this, her body became pliant in his arms, her lips soft, her heart and soul joyous.

When Joshua ended the kiss, she couldn't see him in sharp focus for a sensuous haze obscured her vision like a pure white gauze curtain filtering strong sunlight.

"So, will you promise to do anything for me if I release that account to you?"

Her vision cleared. She couldn't have heard him right. "What? What did you just say?" Kaya asked.

"You heard me."

Using both hands to break free from his embrace, Kaya glowered at him. "You…you beast. Just when I thought there might be some decency in you, some kindness, you act like an arrogant, selfish, conceited Cunningham." She ran into the bathroom and locked the door.

"Kaya, come out and talk to me."

She turned the shower on full blast to drown out the sound of his voice and the sound of her sobs.

Chapter Four

When Joshua returned to the house early that afternoon, he went straight upstairs to Kaya's room. The moment he entered it, he knew she had left the ranch. Just to make sure, he went to check the bathroom. Her underthings were gone. She had locked herself in the bathroom to cry. At least he suspected she'd wept. And the minute he'd left, she'd run away. She probably figured he wouldn't give her the money.

Disappointment surged through him. He hated women who ran off when things didn't go their way. First his mother and now Kaya. Cursing himself for caring, he ran downstairs, hollering for Clancy.

"Hold your horses. I'm coming," Clancy yelled back, bringing in the last of the grocery sacks.

"Where's Kaya?" Joshua demanded.

"Halfway to Abilene would be my guess."

Fixing Clancy with an accusing stare, Joshua said, "You took her to the Crossroads to catch the bus."

"Yup. She's a grown woman, free to come and go."

"Yeah? What if she has a relapse? What if she decides to sue the Diamond C?"

"Miss Kaya ain't the kind of woman who'd do that. If she was, she'd have taken the family for a good-size settlement when you all drove her to divorce Derrick. Seems to me none of you understood her. Or appreciated her. Darn shame, too."

"And you understood her?" Joshua asked, his voice caustic.

"Better'n you."

Joshua shook his head. "She sure has taken you in. A woman who didn't even come to her own husband's funeral."

"She did come," Clancy said, calmly putting canned goods into the cupboard.

"She told you that and you believed her?"

"I generally believe what I see with my own eyes."

"What are you saying? Clancy, if you don't stop putting those canned tomatoes away, I'll throw them out the window!"

Clancy faced Joshua squarely. "On the way back from Derrick's funeral, I noticed I didn't have my pocket watch. I thought I might have lost it in the cemetery, so I drove back. Everybody was gone, except one person. She was hardly more than a slip of a girl, kneelin' by the grave, cryin' so hard I thought she might choke on her tears. I thought I'd give her some grievin' time before I spoke to her. But then the funeral guys came to cover the grave. She ran to a rattletrap car parked on the road and drove off before I had a chance to talk to her. And that's God's truth."

"Why didn't you tell us this?" Joshua demanded.

"Who should I have told? Ray was ready to die. You, I figured didn't care. And Lily? She'd have thrown one of her fits, and I wasn't hankerin' to have her jump all over me."

"I wish I'd known." Joshua rubbed his hand wearily

over his eyes. Then he went to his office. He dialed the number of the private detective he used to run background checks on prospective employees. The conversation was short and to the point. Before long, he'd know everything about Kaya.

Two days later, the detective reported to Joshua.

"She's taken a second job?" Joshua asked with a frown.

"In a cocktail lounge. The ABC Club," the detective said.

"What kind of place is this?"

"Nice. Upscale clientele. Don't water their drinks."

Joshua wrote down the address of the club. "What else?"

"Ms. Cunningham bought groceries and took them to a duplex not far from her apartment. A guy came to the door and took them from her."

"What did the guy look like?"

"Middle twenties, black hair, black mustache, muscular build. Women probably consider him good-looking."

Joshua didn't like that description at all. What was Kaya doing taking groceries to some young stud?

"There's more. She went to the hospital."

"Is she ill?" Joshua asked, unable to keep his concern out of his voice.

"No. She went in with a gift-wrapped package during visiting hours."

"Any idea who she visited?"

"Yes. A little girl by the name of Natalie Cunningham."

Joshua sat as if struck by lightning. Kaya had a daughter? Of all the possibilities for her needing money he'd thought about, this was one that never occurred to him. Where was the girl's father? Was the father that worthless creep who let Kaya buy groceries for him? Recovering from his shock, Joshua asked, "How old is this child?"

"I wasn't able to find that out, but the nurse I talked to referred to Natalie as 'a sweet little girl.'" The detective waited a beat. "Is there anything else I can do?"

"That's all for now. Thanks."

Clancy entered the office, carrying a cup of coffee. "What's wrong?" he asked. "You look like you've been kicked by a mule."

"Kaya has a daughter. A little girl who's in the hospital."

"No wonder she was anxious to get back to Abilene. Miss Kaya wasn't wearin' no wedding ring. Is there a husband?"

"She said she wasn't married now."

"I wonder where the little girl's daddy is. Bet the son of a gun took off and left 'em to fend for themselves. Boy, I'd love to get my hands on that sorry excuse for a man." Clancy paused. "I bet the child's name is Natalie."

Joshua stared at Clancy. "How did you know?"

"Miss Kaya said the name when she was delirious. She also said another name. Yours."

"You sure?" Joshua was startled and then pleased.

"I'm sure. Why did she come back to the ranch?"

The pleasure Joshua felt vanished. "Money, what else?"

"Did you give it to her?"

"No."

"What? Of all—"

"Hold on. I didn't know she had a child. Besides, she refused to tell me why she needed the money. Don't you think I'd have given it to her if I'd known about her sick child?"

"I wonder why she didn't tell you about Natalie. She must have had her reasons." Clancy thought for a moment.

"I bet Miss Kaya's a good mother. Unlike some women I've known."

"Who're you talking about?" Joshua asked with a frown.

"Not your mama. She was a good woman. A good mother—"

"Clancy! We don't talk about her in this house."

"Damn shame," Clancy muttered. Seeing Joshua's expression, he added quickly, "I was talkin' about Lily. That surprise you?"

Joshua shrugged. "She loved Derrick."

"She did, but love ain't enough. Kids need discipline and limits. Lily spoiled him. Spoiled him rotten." Clancy lifted a hand to forestall Joshua's outburst. "I know you don't like to hear nothin' said against your half brother. I'm not sayin' it was his fault. It was Lily's. Anyway, that's old history." Puzzled, he added, "I wonder why Miss Kaya didn't tell us about Natalie."

"Maybe because she's using Cunningham as the girl's last name. That bothers me. She has no right to give Derrick's name to some other man's child."

"We don't know why she did it. Or who the child's daddy is. Wait to hear her side of the story before you do anything," Clancy pleaded.

"Oh, I'll hear her side all right. That woman owes me an explanation. And it better be a good one."

Kaya glanced at the clock behind the bar. It was almost eleven. She could leave in a few minutes and not a moment too soon for her feet felt like they were stuck in solid iron shoes with burning soles. Still, the pay at the ABC Club was good and the tips she'd received were generous. Now, if she could only keep up her strength and stamina, her financial situation should improve quickly.

Five minutes later she was on her way. She had discovered a shortcut to her apartment. Although it took her through a deserted stretch of warehouses and empty buildings, Kaya kept her doors locked and thus felt fairly safe. Tonight, though, a car followed her through a yellow traffic light and stayed with her whether she speeded up or slowed down. Considering her options, she decided to make a run for it.

Once she got to her apartment, she would be all right. The houses were built close enough together that someone would hear her scream. The pursuit car was almost in her back seat. Nearing her apartment, she formulated her strategy. She would hit the brake at the last minute, just in time to pull up in front of the house. The pursuer would be forced to drive on and park farther down the street. That would give her time to run inside.

The plan would have worked except her pursuer didn't park down the street. He stopped his car in front of hers, leaving its rear end sticking way out into the street. By the time she reached her front fender, he was coming toward her. With the streetlight behind him, he looked big.

She was opening her mouth to scream, when she recognized him. "You! What's the matter with you? You almost scared me to death."

With his hands on his hips, Joshua glowered at her. "I meant to scare you. Have you lost your mind, taking that route home? What if your car broke down? Do you have any idea what kind of men would be likely to show up in that part of town?"

"My car won't break down again. Mike fixed it, remember?"

"I suppose you have it in writing from on high that it won't break down again? It's not exactly a new car now, is it?"

"Why were you following me?" she asked, ignoring his remarks about her car.

"I want to talk to you, but not in the middle of the street. Invite me up to your apartment, Kaya."

"How do you know my apartment is upstairs?"

"A lucky guess. Can I come up?" When she hesitated, he asked, "Are you afraid to be alone with me?"

"Not on your best day, Joshua Cunningham. Come on up." His arrogant male challenge, issued in velvety tones, had tricked her into extending the invitation.

"Thanks. I won't stay long."

When he started to follow her, she asked, "Are you going to leave your car parked like that?"

"I'll park it properly, but you wait for me right here."

A few minutes later they walked into her apartment in silence. Kaya preceded him, snapping on a single lamp. She couldn't remember if anything of Natalie's was in the living room, but with the light dim, he might not notice if there was. With a sigh of relief, she stepped out of her shoes.

Joshua looked around the room. "Nice. Comfortable. But do you always live like a mole?"

"No point in turning on more lights. You're not staying long, and I'm going to crawl into bed right after a quick shower to get rid of the cigarette smoke and the smell of liquor clinging to me."

"I'm surprised you took a job in a cocktail lounge since you don't like liquor."

"There aren't that many evening jobs around that pay good money." Then the implication of his question hit her. "How did you know about the club?"

"It doesn't matter how I found out about the ABC Club. Why do you need money so urgently? Doesn't look to me as if you live above your income," Joshua said, slowly walking around the room, examining its contents. He picked up a painted ceramic cat.

Kaya grabbed the Mexican knickknack from his hand and put it down.

He paused in front of the small rug hanging on the wall. "Nice. An heirloom?"

"Yes. One of my Hopi ancestors made it. What do you mean, it doesn't matter how you knew? It matters to me. Have you been spying on me?" she asked, following him as he resumed his curious prowling through her living room.

"Why, do you have something to hide?" he asked in a deceptively casual voice. He touched the piñata suspended from the ceiling.

"I don't believe what I'm hearing. You hired someone to follow me didn't you? I'd have noticed that tank you drive if it had been following me."

"Now you're insulting my car," he said, picking up a children's book.

Kaya snatched it out of his hand and stuck it under a pile of library books. "Darn it, don't evade my question. Did you hire a private detective? That is the usual Cunningham style isn't it? Lily hired one in an attempt to dig up some dirt on me when Derrick and I got married. Did you know that? Of course you did. That's probably where you got the idea. Answer me, please."

"As soon as you answer my questions." Joshua grabbed her by her shoulders. He'd meant only to stop her from turning away, but somehow he ended up pulling her against him.

Instantly every nerve ending in Kaya's body jumped on

the alert. A little of what she felt was anxiety, but most of it was excitement. Giddy excitement.

Their eyes met and held. Joshua's expression was a little surprised. The slight hitch in his breathing banished the last whisper of cold reason. With his fingers pressed against her neck, Joshua urged her closer, his gaze never leaving hers. When she didn't resist, except for a low murmur that could have been as much encouragement as halfhearted protest, he kissed her.

His scent, his touch, his taste, rushed through her, took possession of her. She yielded even as she wondered how this could be happening to her. It couldn't. With the last remnant of willpower, Kaya broke the kiss. She sighed and leaned her head on Joshua's shoulder. She had meant to escape his arms immediately, but that seemed to be beyond her physical ability. She needed a few seconds to regain her strength. At the moment she couldn't even feel her feet, though she assumed they hadn't been consumed by the heat that raged through her and were still attached to the rest of her body.

This was insane. How could she be attracted to Joshua Cunningham? The man didn't like her. He spied on her. How could she respond to him so wholeheartedly? She had lost what good sense she used to have, that's why. And how could he kiss her as if that kiss meant something to him? She knew it didn't. He was reacting to this unexpected, ridiculous chemistry between them. The thought allowed strength and reason to return. Kaya freed herself and moved away.

"I'm thirsty. You want some iced tea or water?" she asked, walking toward the kitchen. Her voice had been whispery weak, which she hated.

"A glass of water would be nice." Joshua followed her to the kitchen. He accepted the glass she handed him with fingers that weren't quite steady.

"Thanks. It's turned hot, hasn't it?" he murmured, and wiped perspiration from his forehead.

"Yes, it has," she agreed, brushing back a strand of hair that had escaped the comb holding it smoothly against her head.

Joshua seemed to be observing her carefully. It took all of her concentration not to fidget.

"Are you going to answer my question?" she asked.

"What was it?"

"Whether you hired a private detective to find me?"

"I did."

His ready admission left her silent and wide-eyed with surprise.

"What?" Joshua asked.

"I can't believe you would admit something like that without batting an eye. Aren't you the least bit ashamed of stooping to this…this underhanded technique?"

"No, because there's nothing underhanded about it. The man I hired is in the business of finding lost or missing things. It's perfectly legitimate." The instant these words left his mouth, Joshua knew he was in trouble. "You look like a cat whose fur has been stroked the wrong way. I didn't mean to upset you."

"First of all, I'm not a 'thing' and second, I wasn't lost or missing." She shook her head. "You Cunninghams sure have a cavalier way of looking at the rest of the world."

"I suppose it might seem that way, but the truth is that money makes a lot of things possible and legitimate. That's the way of the world, Kaya."

Remembering her large, unpaid hospital bills, she said wistfully, "Must be nice."

"Sometimes." Joshua shrugged. "It also has its drawbacks."

She flicked him a disbelieving look. "Such as?"

"People wanting things from you. Buttering you up for that reason. Makes it hard to know for sure who your real friends are. As for women…." Joshua made a dismissing gesture and drained his glass. Crossing his arms over his chest, he said, "I've answered your question. Now answer mine. Why do you need money so desperately?"

"It's not for a lover, if that's what you're wondering." When Joshua didn't say anything, but waited with an expectant expression, she added, "Isn't that answer enough for you?"

"No." He waited, giving her a chance to tell the truth.

"All I can tell you is that the money won't be spent on anything frivolous or useless."

"No, groceries aren't frivolous or useless."

Something in his tone indicted that there was more to that seemingly matter-of-fact statement. "What are you talking about?"

"The groceries you took to a…how did the P.I. put it? A young stud down the street?"

Kaya stared at him uncomprehendingly. Then the truth hit her. "You mean Manny? Oh, for crying out loud! That's Maria's husband. And Maria is my cousin."

"All right, so I was wrong about that. Why don't you tell me the truth then? Why don't you tell me about your daughter in the hospital?"

The empty glass slid from Kaya's fingers. She didn't notice that it shattered when it hit the tile floor.

"Kaya?" When she didn't respond, but stood as if in shock, he called her name again.

Her worst nightmare was coming true. The Cunninghams had found out about Natalie. They might take her daughter. No, not take probably, but Lily might want to visit. Subject Natalie to that vicious tongue of hers. Kaya felt ill. The room swayed. Fear paralyzed Kaya's voice.

"Kaya?" When she took a step forward, Joshua reached out and laid a hand on her shoulder. "Don't move," he ordered. "You're in your stocking feet. You'll cut yourself on the glass." Placing his hands on either side of her waist, he lifted her up onto the countertop. "Stay there. Where do you keep your broom and dustpan?"

Kaya pointed to the utility room. Part of her mind was aware that Joshua fetched the broom and swept the floor. Part of her mind raced desperately to find a way to keep her daughter. What in heaven's name could she do? Why couldn't she think straight?

When Joshua finished sweeping, she jumped down. He came to stand before her. She couldn't look at him. Not yet. She concentrated on his boots. Hand-sewn black boots that cost the earth.

Joshua placed his hand under her chin to raise her face before he spoke. "Kaya, why didn't you tell me you needed money for your sick child? Why the secrecy?"

Because if you knew she was a real flesh-and-blood Cunningham you might take her from me, or worse. Lily might want a hand in raising her. Destroy my sweet child's self-confidence. Call her ugly names until she feels less than nothing.

"It's no sin to have a baby and not be married. Illegitimacy is no longer a disgrace."

What was Joshua talking about? Illegitimacy? What did he mean?

"Did your lover run off and leave you when he found out you were pregnant? Is that what happened?"

Slowly a glimmer of what he was saying broke through Kaya's shock-numbed senses. Joshua didn't know that his brother was Natalie's father. There was still a chance to keep her child. Hope seeped back into her heart.

"Is Natalie's father dead?"

"Yes," Kaya said without hesitation as it was the truth.

"I'm sorry. It must have been hard for you. How old is your daughter?"

Something odd was going on here. How much did Joshua know? Kaya studied his face. It showed concern but not the emotions she thought he would feel if he suspected the truth. She had to find out exactly what he knew.

"How did you find out about my daughter?" she asked, her voice still shaky.

"The private detective followed you to the hospital."

"Did he see Natalie?"

"No. He talked to one of the aides."

"What did she tell him about Natalie?"

"Not much. Her name and that she was your little girl."

Relief flooded through Kaya, making her weak-kneed. She longed to sit down, but Joshua's hand still rested against her chin. She wasn't sure he'd let her move away if she tried. Moreover, he might construe her attempt to get away from him as a sign of weakness or of guilt. Kaya forced herself to stand very still.

Joshua had no inkling of who Natalie's father was, thank God. If she played this right, he would leave and still not know the truth. Joshua was no fool, though. She had to be careful and clever. If only she were a better actress. But with what was at stake, she was going to give an academy-award performance or die trying.

"One thing I don't understand. Why did you give her Derrick's name? Since she isn't his daughter, she isn't entitled to it. Why? Were you planning to cash in on the Cunningham name?"

Careful how you answer that, Kaya cautioned herself. *Don't blurt out the truth no matter how much Joshua riles you.* "No, I hadn't planned on cashing in on the Cunningham name. If I could have paid the hospital bills, I would never have contacted you. I hadn't planned on ever seeing you or the Diamond C again."

For some inexplicable reason her answer seemed to upset him deeply. She could see his jaws working as he bit down hard.

"That still doesn't explain why you're passing off your illegitimate daughter as a Cunningham. You have no right to do that."

Now she understood and was crushed. She'd always thought that Joshua was the one Cunningham to whom her ethnic background and social standing didn't matter. How wrong she'd been. She bit the inside of her cheek to keep the tears of bitter disillusionment from rising into her eyes.

"Talk to me, Kaya."

How could she? She couldn't tell him the truth, and anything less would sound unconvincing. Still, she had to come up with some answer. Joshua didn't look as if he were about to leave without an explanation. Kaya hated lies, yet she seemed to be doing nothing but lying every time she saw him. She'd stick as close to the truth as she could. That was the best she could do.

"It's very simple. I'd kept my married name, so it was natural that I gave it to my daughter, too. There was no devious plan to cash in on the high and mighty Cunningham name. That never occurred to me."

"Why did you keep Derrick's name? You rejected him easily enough, so why not reject his name as well?"

"Did anybody ever tell you that your voice can get mean enough to strip the skin off a person's back?" she asked.

"It's been mentioned. Answer my question."

The anger she'd kept a tight rein on exploded. "You have a nerve! You hire a private eye to spy on me, you follow me and scare me half to death, and then you interrogate me in my apartment with the skill a CIA agent might envy! Is that what growing up with wealth and power does to a person? Well, then I'm glad my daughter will grow up in poverty and love."

Undeterred by her outburst and her fiery green eyes, Joshua asked again, "Why did you keep Derrick's name?"

Kaya threw her hands up in total frustration, forcing him to release her. "Oh God, help me! You're nothing if not persistent." She closed her eyes, willing herself to calm down. Then, with resignation in her voice, she said, "All right, I'll tell you. Not because you've a right to know, but because it's midnight, and I've worked two jobs today and will work two jobs tomorrow. I'm tired, and I want you out of here." She stopped to take another deep breath.

"I kept the Cunningham name because I was entitled to it and because Lily didn't want me to keep it. She tried so hard to get the marriage declared illegal, I wasn't about to let her do it even when it was over. She'd won everything else, including my husband. Call it sheer perverseness or whatever you will, but that was my reason and nothing else."

Joshua nodded. "I can understand that. Lily has that effect on people. And speaking of my stepmother, are you going to be as possessive and controlling with your daughter as Lily was with Derrick?"

Horror caused Kaya to shiver. "May God strike me dead on the spot if I am."

"Perhaps you mean that," Joshua murmured. "Clancy is convinced you're a good mother. Tell me, what's wrong with your little girl?"

"She's got aplastic anemia. Not a severe case, thank God, but she caught pneumonia. With her white blood count down, her body has a hard time fighting a severe infection like that."

"Anemia? That's a blood disorder."

Joshua's expression was thoughtful, as if he was searching his memory for something. Kaya's protective senses picked up on that as efficiently as a submarine's sonar picked up sound. Whatever it was he was wondering about, she sensed that it posed a threat to Natalie and her. She had to distract him.

"Joshua, I don't mean to be rude, but it's getting late."

"Are you throwing me out?"

"Yes."

The cloisonné comb was slipping down her glossy black hair. Joshua reached out to remove it. He lifted her heavy hair, letting it slide through his fingers.

"What's with all this touching?" Kaya demanded, but her voice wasn't nearly as firm as she'd intended it to be. "Is this another one of your ploys? What are you after?"

"No ploy. And you know damned well what this is about. That ancient man-woman thing is pulling at us so strong we can hardly fight it."

"Oh, yes, we can. I can, and I will. I've had my heart broken by one Cunningham man. I'm not about to make the same mistake again."

"Did anybody ever tell you that those eyes of yours can put a spell on a man? Crack his heart right in half?"

"I don't think you're afraid of a broken heart or a spell."

Joshua grinned at her roguishly. "Maybe not, but you sure can put a man's body into a lot of torment. And if you're truthful, you won't deny that you feel that electric force between us, too."

"I don't deny it," she agreed grudgingly, "but that doesn't mean I'll give in to it. No way. Never."

"Never say never, Kaya."

"I bet you never risked your heart, did you?"

An expression she couldn't interpret crossed his face. He turned away.

"Good night, Kaya."

"Good night, Joshua."

"I'll see you soon."

"What for?" she asked suspiciously.

Still grinning, he said, "You're right. For that male-female thing, too, but also to drop off a cashier's check."

She was so astonished that she watched him leave, unable to say anything. By the time she recovered her voice, she heard him close the downstairs door. She ran to the window and watched him drive off.

"Thank you and bless you, Joshua. You'll never know what this means to me. To Natalie," she whispered.

Chapter Five

With only five hours of restless sleep the night before, Joshua poured himself another cup of coffee, his fourth, in an effort to rouse himself to a state of full alertness.

Clancy slanted a look at Josh's morose expression from time to time as he prepared a roast for the oven.

"Why didn't you sleep longer? The morning's shot anyway and a couple more hours might have made you easier to live with," Clancy said after a long silence. When Josh ignored this statement, Clancy couldn't contain his curiosity any longer. "Now that you've finished the pot of coffee, you'd better tell me what you found out about Miss Kaya and her little girl."

Joshua rubbed his hand over his eyes and then over his unshaven chin. Of the two, he didn't know which felt more scratchy. "Didn't find out much," he muttered. "She sure is closemouthed about her daughter."

"What about the child's daddy?"

"Kaya says he's dead."

Clancy heard the doubt in Josh's voice. "You don't believe that?"

Joshua shrugged. "She's not telling the truth, at least not all of it."

Clancy chewed on that for a while before he asked, "What's wrong with the little girl?"

"She's got some kind of blood disorder. Aplastic anemia." Joshua sensed rather than saw Clancy's hand pause above the roast. Looking at Clancy, he asked, "What?"

Clancy put the pepper shaker down. "That's odd. Mighty odd."

"What is?"

"Remember when Derrick was little and he had that spell of anemia that took him a long time to get over? Wasn't that what he had?"

"Yeah." Now Joshua knew what had been nagging at him ever since Kaya told him about Natalie's illness. "What a coincidence," he muttered thoughtfully, "and you know I don't believe in coincidences." A thought flitted through his mind that gave him pause. No, it couldn't be. If Natalie were Derrick's daughter, Kaya would have asked for help years ago. Wouldn't she? Of course, she would have. Anybody would have. He dismissed the thought.

Clancy shook his head. "Here we go for years without hearin' nothin' about that kind of anemia and when we do, it's somebody we know who's got it. That's strange." Clancy shook his head again. "Poor Miss Kaya. How's she gonna manage, working two jobs and takin' care of her little girl when she gets out of the hospital? It took a heap of nursin' when Derrick came home, remember?"

"I'm releasing the money in the special account to Kaya. That should help."

Clancy nodded and sent Josh an approving, proud look. He didn't say anything, feeling it was unnecessary to do so. He expected Josh to do the right thing. He'd been raised to recognize and respect the privileges as well as the responsibilities that went with wealth and power. Clancy had seen to that.

"How soon you gonna give her the money?"

"Tomorrow."

"You gonna visit the little girl in the hospital?"

"I was thinking about it." That far-fetched idea snaked through his brain again.

"Go visit the little girl," Clancy urged. "Miss Kaya will appreciate knowin' that we're thinkin' of her, I'm sure. I'm gonna bake my special chocolate cake. I want you to take a couple of pieces with you when you go. You know what hospital's food is like." Clancy shuddered.

Joshua spent the rest of the morning in his office, updating the ranch records. He must have made errors in entering the figures because the numbers on the screen made no sense. His mind wasn't on his work, but on his beautiful ex-sister-in-law. With an oath he shut off the machine. He needed work. Real work, cowboy work, not this tapping on keys that were too small for his fingers.

Kaya hummed as she drove to the hospital. She couldn't remember the last time she'd felt this lighthearted. That's what the prospect of paying off the hospital bill did for her. She wouldn't quit her second job though, until that bill was marked Paid In Full. Not that she doubted Joshua's promise of releasing the money to her. He was undoubtedly capable of many things, but breaking his word wasn't one of them.

With all her heart Kaya wished she could take several weeks off and nurse her daughter until she was ready to start school. But that much money she couldn't save, unfortunately. Her cousin would take good care of Natalie. Kaya knew that, but it wasn't the same. She longed to do it herself.

Kaya sighed. It did no good to wish for things. Hadn't she learned that life didn't often grant wishes? Or if it did, life didn't grant them for long. Like Derrick. She'd wanted him as she'd never wanted anything before in her young life. He'd been hers for such a short, short time. And what a price she'd had to pay for that brief happiness.

She shook her head in an effort to dislodge those painful memories. Life had forced her to shelve her dreams. At least until recently, until she'd met Joshua again. He and her trip to the Diamond C had vividly revived the past. But she didn't want to dwell on the events. Moreover, she didn't have the strength or the time to do so. She needed to stay focused on Natalie.

Kaya parked her car, took the small present she'd made for Natalie and entered the hospital.

Pausing outside Natalie's room, Kaya heard a man's voice. The low, melodic voice teased at her familiarly. It couldn't be, Kaya thought. It sounded like Joshua's voice because she'd been thinking about the man almost nonstop. Natalie had to be watching television. Lots of actors had that sort of caressing voice.

When she pushed the door open wider, she stopped as if turned to stone on the spot. She felt her blood draining from her face, from her heart, from her body. Blindly she groped for the door and then clung to it to keep upright.

"Mommy! Joshua's reading me a story," Natalie called out with a happy smile.

Mutely Kaya stared at the man sitting by her daughter's bed, as if he were a two-headed, four-horned devil. Kaya tried to speak, but her voice seemed frozen. Besides, even if she could have spoken, what did a person say when her world had just crashed around her?

Joshua stared back at her, his gaze unreadable. Except it was empty of warmth, of kindness.

"Mommy? You look funny. Are you going to throw up? Shall I press the button for the nurse?"

She must look as ill as she felt, Kaya thought, when Joshua got up and walked toward her. She barely kept herself from shrinking back against the door.

"You do look pale. Guilt does have that effect on people, I've heard," he said very softly.

His tone was civil on the surface, but Kaya heard the hard edge in it. Joshua clamped his hand around her upper arm.

"What are you doing here?" Kaya asked, her voice barely rising above a whisper.

"I'm a temporary volunteer reader." He pressed her arm again for emphasis. "Join us," he said with deceptive mildness.

She had no choice but to follow him. Not that she would have left him alone with Natalie, but she would have preferred to approach the bed without his help.

"Mommy, look. Joshua brought us each a piece of cake. Clancy baked it. He's a cowboy on Joshua's ranch."

So, he was already working on buying her daughter's affections with bribes. The first step in spoiling her? In turning her into an undisciplined, irresponsible person? Not while she had a single breath left! Kaya recovered her speech and the control over her body. First she pulled free from Joshua's grasp. Then she walked to the other side of Natalie's bed and kissed her daughter.

"How are you today, sweetie?"

"My head doesn't hurt. Dr. Reiger said my new medicine is working. I can go home pretty soon."

"Oh, that's wonderful." With tears in her eyes Kaya hugged Natalie. "I can't wait to get you back home. Look, I brought you another picture."

"Oh, isn't he a pretty color?" Natalie looked at the picture of the golden retriever with shining eyes.

"You collect photos of dogs?" Joshua asked, shooting Kaya a questioning look.

"Until I can have a dog. Mommy says as soon as we have saved some money, we'll live in a little house and then I can have a dog of my own."

Joshua kept flicking her those baleful glances as if she'd just been nominated worst mother of the year. She lifted her chin challengingly and stared right back at him.

"What kind of dog would you like?" Joshua asked.

"I don't care. Mommy says we should adopt a pet from the human society and save his life."

"Humane society," Kaya corrected gently.

"Yeah. That's where animals go who have no home," Natalie told Joshua. "Are you going to finish reading the story?"

"Please do," Kaya said, when Joshua looked at her. While he read she could pull herself together for the coming confrontation with him. Kaya noticed that Natalie listened even more intently than the little girl usually did. She couldn't blame her. Joshua's voice had magic in it. The Pied Piper must have exerted that kind of hypnotic pull on his audience.

Although Joshua hadn't indicated that he knew the truth about Natalie, Kaya suspected that he'd guessed. But maybe he hadn't. Maybe she still could bluff her way through this. Maybe not all was lost.

Joshua closed the book. "Tell me, Natalie, when is your birthday?"

Kaya's heart stopped for a beat. Then it hammered so loudly in her chest that she had to strain to hear Natalie's answer. Joshua would have to be a math illiterate not to figure out who the child's father was.

Their glances met above Natalie's head, Joshua's smoldering with a mixture of joy and anger, Kaya's glittering with false bravado.

"Natalie, I told you that you and I had the same last name, and I told you I owned the ranch where your mother was when she had the flu. What I didn't tell you was that we're related."

There it was, out in the open. Kaya's body swayed as if she had been struck from on high. She held her breath, waiting for Natalie's reaction. In the silence that followed Joshua's portentous announcement, the little girl's glances flew expectantly between the two adults.

"Kaya, you want to tell your daughter who I am?"

"No!" The word exploded from Kaya's mouth involuntarily.

Joshua glowered at her through narrowed eyes. Then he smiled, but the smile was falser than a crocodile's tears. "Surely you want to reconsider that, don't you?" he asked with forced amiability.

Natalie looked at her mother with questioning eyes. Kaya had no choice. Moistening her dry lips with her tongue, she had to start twice before her voice obeyed her. "This is your uncle. Your daddy's brother. Joshua Cunningham."

"You knew my daddy?" Natalie's blue eyes looked enormous with surprise and her voice was tinged with disbelieving awe.

"Sure did. Knew him from the day he was born."

"I never knowed him," Natalie said. "He died and went to heaven before I was born."

Kaya stroked her daughter's hair comfortingly.

"And you didn't know you had an uncle Joshua?" he asked.

Natalie shook her head.

"Well, you do."

Joshua shot Kaya another look that promised a flood of accusatory words. Nor did she like the possessive sound of his voice. The fears she'd tried to hold at bay, rushed at her full force.

The aide came into the room, carrying Natalie's supper tray.

"What's for dessert?" Natalie asked.

"Fruit Jell-O," the aide said.

"I've got chocolate cake."

"Girl, don't tell me that you'd rather eat cake than this wiggly orange stuff I got?" the aide teased.

Kaya listened with only half an ear to the friendly exchange between her daughter and the aide. She had to make plans. She should probably hire a lawyer. Had she ever done anything that could conceivably be considered as poor mothering? Kaya couldn't think of anything, except maybe the fact that she had two jobs. Some judge might consider that as not spending enough time with her daughter and might hold that against the mother.

"Mommy, are you going to eat your cake now?"

"No, sweetie. I'll take it with me." Kaya doubted that she could get anything past her tight throat into her stomach where anxiety had taken up residence and gnawed at her like a starving rat.

"Time to go," Joshua said, touching Kaya's arm.

If only she could get away from him until she could decide on a strategy.

"I'll walk out with you," he said as if he'd guessed her intention to evade him.

Kaya said goodbye to Natalie with a kiss and a hug, took her cake, and walked out of the room. Joshua was right behind her.

"Don't even think of bolting," Joshua warned in a low voice.

"With my daughter here, do you really think I'd run?"

"Running is your usual style, isn't it?" he asked, not bothering to soften the condemnation in his voice.

"You're lucky there are people all around us," Kaya said through clenched teeth. "Right now I'd gladly… Oh, never mind."

He was so close she could feel his slacks brush against her legs. It irritated the living daylights out of her. "And why are you sticking to me like a shadow?" she asked when they reached the parking lot.

"Because I don't trust you not to disappear before we've had a chance to talk."

"I don't want to talk to you."

"I just bet you don't! But guess what? For once you're not getting your way, sweetheart."

"What?" Kaya stopped so suddenly, Joshua had to grab her to keep from falling over her. "Getting my way? I resent your implications that I'm some spoiled woman who always gets her way. What a ridiculous idea!"

"During the past six years you've been on your own, getting your own way, haven't you?" Though he'd regained his balance, he kept his hands firmly cupped over her shoulders.

Kaya stared at Joshua as if he'd completely lost his mind. "Oh, I love your notion of me getting my way. Yes, I got my way in choosing which of the minimum-wage jobs I wanted to take, in which rickety old building I wanted to rent a room, which bill I wanted to pay and which to hold till the next paycheck. Oh, yes. I've had it all my way!"

"If your eyes could incinerate me, I'd be nothing but a pile of ashes on the ground," Joshua observed. Without conscious volition his hold on her tightened.

"Cunningham, get your hands off me! Now. Don't you dare manhandle me."

"Manhandle? If you think this is manhandling, I have news for you." Something in her stance, her demeanor, reminded him of a skittish mare frightened enough to injure herself in a panic. After a second's hesitation, Joshua released her.

With hands braced against her hips, she demanded, "How dare you go to my daughter's room? How dare you intrude into our lives?"

Joshua gaped at her, speechless for once.

"Nobody invited you to become Natalie's uncle. We were doing just fine without any Cunningham relatives."

"How dare I? How dare *you* keep my niece's existence from me?"

"Easy. The Cunninghams didn't want me then, and I don't want them now. Is that so hard to understand?" When Joshua didn't respond but simply looked at her, she added, her voice hard as steel, "I don't care what I have to do, but you're not getting a chance to spoil my daughter. You will not turn her into a spoiled, irresponsible brat." Kaya turned and ran to her car.

Joshua was so dumbfounded by her words that he lost

valuable seconds before he started after her. When he reached her car, she was already behind the wheel, starting the engine.

"Kaya, we have to talk."

"Not now. I have to go to work." She put the car into gear. Looking at his stubborn stance, she warned, "Joshua, get out of my way or I'll run over you, so help me God. I will."

For a moment he remained standing in front of her car. They glowered at each other. Unexpectedly Joshua felt a touch of admiration for her raw courage.

"I believe you'd do it," he muttered, stepping aside. "But we will talk. Make no mistake about that."

He watched her drive away. She was angry, but beneath that anger he sensed something else. Suddenly he realized what that other emotion was: fear. Kaya was afraid of him. Afraid that he might take her daughter? That he might be a bad influence on her? How could she think he'd do something that monstrous? Joshua ran his large hand through his hair in frustration.

True, he was furious with Kaya for keeping Derrick's child from him, but that was a long way from taking her. How could she think he'd tear a child from its mother's arms? He who knew firsthand how painful it was to grow up without a mother? He'd have to prove to that green-eyed beauty once and for all that he was not the monster she imagined him to be.

"Two drafts and a g-and-t." Kaya called to the bartender. While she waited for the order, her eyes surveyed the dimly lit, smoky club. She was grateful for the noisy crowd demanding service. At least while she was taking and delivering drinks she was prevented from reliving that awful moment when she'd caught sight of Joshua sitting at Natalie's bedside. But while she waited for the orders, she wasn't so lucky. Her thoughts circled endlessly around Joshua and what devious schemes he might be hatching. Her heart pounded in anxiety.

What was he planning to do? If she begged and pleaded would he keep Natalie's existence a secret from Lily? She knew he wasn't overly fond of his stepmother, but his fierce family loyalty might override his dislike. The thought of Natalie with Lily was unendurable. It was like a killing blight hanging over a delicate flower.

Kaya picked up and delivered the drinks. On her way back to the bar, a masculine hand snaked out of the booth she passed and grabbed her arm. She swung around, ready to crown the forward male with a blistering remark. When she saw who it was, the words died on her lips. She stood as if transfixed.

The low light of the bar softened the sharp angles of Joshua's face but did not obscure the determined set of his jaw. Kaya had hoped not to have to face him so soon again, but she should have known it wasn't in his stubborn nature to wait or to grant reprieves. The Cunninghams were not renowned for their patience or their tolerance.

"It's you. Just like that proverbial bad penny," she said in her unfriendliest voice.

"Now is that the way to talk to a customer?" Joshua asked. He released her wrist.

She flicked him a look from hostile green eyes that could have withered a patch of poison ivy. It didn't bother him.

"Not only a customer but a relative?"

"Didn't it ever occur to you that not everybody is overjoyed at meeting up with an uppity Cunningham?"

"Careful, Kaya. You're a Cunningham, too."

"Ha! Better not let Lily hear you say that. She's liable to haul off and slap your face."

Joshua shrugged dismissingly. "Lily doesn't worry me, but you do."

"What do you want here anyway?" she demanded.

"You have the nerve to ask me that? What I want, what you owe me, is a long talk and an explanation which had better be good. Real good. But this isn't the time or the place, so I'll settle for a draft beer."

Not bothering to acknowledge his request, she stomped off to the safety of the bar where she lingered, trying to calm herself, until the bartender asked her what she needed. Kaya picked up the glass of beer he drew for her, marched back to Joshua's booth and plunked the beer down in front of him so hard that some of it spilled. With a raised eyebrow he used the cocktail napkin to mop up the liquid.

"You get off at eleven, right?" Joshua remarked.

"Why do you ask when you already know the answer?"

"You sure are grumpy tonight." When he saw her reaction, he added, "Never mind. I'll see you in twenty minutes. I'll wait outside for you."

Kaya walked away without a word, her back stiff with tension.

Joshua watched her. He wouldn't put it past her to try to sneak out and evade him. Five minutes before it was time for her to leave, he went to the parking lot. Leaning against the door of her car, he waited for her.

When she saw him, Kaya muttered, "I'd hoped you'd be gone, but no such luck, I see."

"I told you we'd have a talk. Why would you think I'd change my mind?"

"I'd hoped you might have a sudden attack of kindness."

"Kindness?" he asked as if the word were Sanskrit instead of English.

"Yeah, you know when people are nice to someone who's been hit emotionally with a nail-studded two-by-four?"

"I know the meaning of the word," he said dryly. "And you're not the only one who's been hit by a two-by-four. How do you think I feel finding out after all these years that I have a niece?"

When Kaya remained silent, he said, "You mentioned kindness. Why didn't you practice a little of it while my dad was still alive? Don't you think Ray would have loved knowing he had a grandchild on the way before he died? Don't you think that might have made the loss of his son and his own impending death a little easier to take? That would have been kindness."

"Oh, get real, Joshua. You all wouldn't even have let me set foot on the Diamond C after the divorce, much less talk to Ray. One of the conditions the attorney made when he offered me that money and brought the divorce papers was that I was not ever to go back to the ranch. Or have you forgotten that? You'd probably have sicced that bad tempered Brahman bull on me."

"You can't sic a bull on someone," Joshua corrected automatically. "And I didn't know about the no-visit clause."

Kaya made a disbelieving sound. Facing the car, she slumped against it. "Look, it's been a bear of a day. I'm tired. I'd like to go home."

"It's probably a better idea to talk about all this in your apartment than right here."

Kaya groaned. She dropped her arms on top of her car's roof and laid her head against them. Her whole body exuded weariness. How small her hands were, how fine-boned her wrists. Almost too fragile to carry the heavy loads they carried. For an instant Joshua felt compassion for her. Then he remembered that she had kept Natalie a secret.

"Kaya?" he prompted.

She sighed deeply before she spoke. "Oh, leave it be, Joshua. What's done is done. The past is over. Can't we just go on with our lives?"

"You'd like that, wouldn't you? Forgive and forget. Well, I can't. Not until everything is clear. I'll follow you to your place. Unless you want to talk about this in my hotel room?"

"No!"

"I didn't think so." Joshua laid his hand against her hair. He could almost feel it crackling with life and energy, even though Kaya was tired. For a moment he wanted to stroke her hair and murmur comforting words. Then he came to his senses. Exerting a little pressure on her neck, he said, "Let's go, Kaya. The sooner we get started, the sooner we'll be done talking and you can get some rest."

She turned. His fingers slid to her throat. She flashed him a cool look. Or as cool a look as she could manage, with his hand resting against her throat. "I thought all cowboys were supposed to be men of few words."

Joshua's mouth twitched. He suppressed a grin. "I'm the exception. I want to hear words from you. Truthful words. Lots of them. Let's go."

Slowly he removed his fingers from her throat where he could feel her pulse beating. How could he be attracted to a woman who made him so mad he wanted to shake her? Thank heaven she didn't realize that if she as much as half tried, she might come close to being able to manipulate him. No other woman had ever been this much of a threat to him. Not even his ex-wife. He'd best be on his guard. Joshua stepped back, fixing her with a stern stare.

"I'm going. I'm going," Kaya said, resigned. She unlocked her car, got in, and drove off.

Joshua followed her. She didn't take the short-cut, he noted. Chalk one up for him. This small sign on her part that she did listen to him, made him a little less upset with her.

She waited for him in front of the duplex. Silently she preceded him into the apartment.

"All right. What do you want to know? Or rather, what is it you want to say to me? What blame, what accusation, what…whatever? Say it and let's get it over with."

"Why don't you take your shoes off? Your feet must be killing you."

Kaya shook her head. "I'm fine. Don't pretend that you're concerned about my well being. We both know you're here only because of Natalie. Just get on with it."

Joshua shrugged. "If that's what you want." He came to stand before her, close enough to touch her. He saw that his nearness caused a flicker of unease in her eyes, but she stood her ground. Silently he saluted her courage.

"First of all, I never saw the agreement the lawyer drew up. All I knew was that the family offered you money. You must believe that."

"Why must I?" she demanded, ready to go the full ten rounds if necessary.

"Because it's the truth. I never knew about the no-visitation clause."

"I wondered why you didn't throw me off the Diamond C when I arrived there the other day. Of course, it helped that Lily wasn't there."

"So you believe me?"

Kaya shrugged. "I imagine the terms of the agreement were dictated primarily by your stepmother. She wouldn't have consulted you. Or anybody else. She loved being a law onto herself. And you all allowed it."

"I didn't have much to say at the time. Dad was still alive and head of the family. At least in name. My guess is that he's the one who insisted that money be provided for you."

Kaya nodded in agreement. "Lily wanted to be rid of me in the worst way. Still, it must have galled her when Ray instructed the attorney to offer me a settlement."

"Did you know you were pregnant when you tore up the check?"

"No. At least not on a conscious level. I should have guessed that I might be, but I was still so upset that I didn't think straight. When the lawyer came with the divorce papers, I was devastated all over again. You see, deep down I still hoped that Derrick would come after me."

"And take you back to a life of luxury?" Joshua asked with a sardonic twist around his mouth.

"No! Oh, what's the use of talking with you! You don't listen. You hear only what you want to hear! You're so filled with Cunningham prejudices that you're incapable of seeing someone else's point of view."

"That's not true, but go on. Why didn't you contact us later, when you were sure of the pregnancy? You must have needed money."

"I certainly did."

"So?" he prompted when she fell silent again.

"So, after I went to the doctor and was sure that I was

pregnant, I was trying to figure the best way to get in touch with Derrick without Lily finding out about it. The next thing I knew, he was dead."

"That shouldn't have stopped you. You were entitled to help from us."

A bitter, brittle sound broke from Kaya's throat that bore only the faintest similarity to laughter. "None of you thought enough of me to call me and tell me about Derrick's death. How do you think I felt when I heard it on the evening news? That one omission showed me as nothing else could how little you all valued me. And don't tell me that you didn't know where I was! Your lawyer had located me, remember?"

With a grim expression, Joshua said, "It was unforgivable of us not to let you know. I'm as guilty as the rest of the family. Derrick's death was such a shock, I didn't think straight. No matter how much I blamed you, no matter how much I resented you for what you did, if I could go back in time—" Joshua broke off, rubbing his hand across his forehead.

"But you can't go back. None of us can."

He studied her lovely, tormented face intently. "There's something else, isn't there? What aren't you telling me?"

Kaya lifted her shoulders in a small shrug and fixed her gaze carefully on the floor.

"Let's see," Joshua said, enumerating the facts as he knew them. "You weren't even eighteen yet when Derrick died. If I remember correctly, you didn't have any family you could turn to. Money ran through Derrick's hands like water through a sieve, so he couldn't have given you much when you left. So there you were, a pregnant teenager without anyone to turn to and without any money. The natural thing to do in the circumstances would have been for you to come to us."

"There was nothing natural in these circumstances," Kaya insisted.

"What were you so afraid of that kept you from contacting us? What did you think Lily would do to you that you'd rather suffer in silence and in poverty than ask for help?"

Kaya turned her back on him. She stared through the window out into the darkness.

"What was it, Kaya?"

"What difference does it make now? None. Leave it alone, Joshua," she said wearily.

Joshua took her arms and turned her to face him. She'd slipped behind that neutral mask again. "You said something to me today that gives me a clue. What was it? Something like 'You can't have my daughter'? That's it. You were afraid that Lily would take her grandchild from you, right?" The mask slipped from her deathly pale face. He saw the naked fear and desperation in her eyes. He saw the truth. It ripped through him like the hard horns of an angry bull.

Kaya shook her head. In a voice ragged with emotion, Kaya said, "I doubt that she'd have wanted custody of the grandchild of that unsuitable girl her son married. What scared me was, and still is, how Lily would treat Natalie. I couldn't bear to have my little girl called the names she used to call me. Be embarrassed and denigrated and made to feel worthless." Kaya shuddered visibly.

"I don't want Lily anywhere near Natalie. I wouldn't entrust a baby worm to Lily's care much less my sweet child. I'll not let Lily treat Natalie the way she treated me—or the way she treated her son. I'll go down fighting, screaming, and bleeding. Do you hear me? I'll die first!" Kaya grabbed Joshua's shirt with both hands and shook him as hard as she could. Tears streamed down her face.

Desperation gave her strength. It took Joshua several seconds before he'd pried her hands loose. He twisted them behind her back as gently as he could and held her against him with his other arm.

"I'm not going to take your daughter or let Lily hurt her. Do you hear me, Kaya? So stop fighting me. I don't want to hurt you. Sh. Sh," he murmured soothingly. She wept with great wrenching sobs that shook her body and tore at his heart, but he let her weep until her sobs stopped and her body slumped against his.

"Nobody is going to hurt Natalie or embarrass her or make her feel inferior," Joshua repeated, his voice rock-hard. He stroked her hair in a gesture meant to be comforting and reassuring. "Lily isn't going to get a chance to influence Natalie in any way. I am going to take care of both of you. I'm going to take you home to the Diamond C."

Kaya's body stiffened with shock. She couldn't have heard him right. "What?" she whispered.

Chapter Six

"I said, I'm going to take both of you home," Joshua repeated, preparing himself for the arguments and the protests he knew she would raise.

Kaya took two steps back. Looking around her, she said, "This is my home. Natalie's home. We've been happy here. We're not going anywhere else."

Joshua glanced at the room.

Seeing his assessing expression, Kaya drew herself up to her full height. "I know this apartment isn't anywhere near as elegant as the designer rooms at the ranch, but it's not a dump either."

"Don't flash those green eyes at me like that. I didn't say it was a dump. Stop anticipating what I'm going to say. You have a habit of doing that. And most of your assumptions about me are wrong."

When Joshua saw her open her mouth to speak, he said, "Let me finish, please. But why live here and pay rent when we have all that room at the ranch? You yourself said that the house was meant for children. Now there's a Cunningham child to fill those rooms."

"No! The ranch's too far. I'd spend every waking minute driving back and forth to work. I'd have no time to spend with Natalie."

"I hadn't meant for you to drive to work every day. Can't you quit your job? You've got to give up your evening job as soon as Natalie is released anyway. If you can hang on that long." Joshua framed her face with his hands. With the thumb of his right hand he touched the sensitive skin below her eye.

"You've got dark circles under your eyes, you look exhausted, and you've lost weight. You're hardly more than skin and bones now." That wasn't strictly true. Joshua could feel some of her curves pressed against him even as he spoke, but she was thinner. He didn't like bony women. He loved those full curves, their tantalizing softness—

"Joshua, are you listening to me?"

"Yes, yes," he lied. "You want to keep your job, but can't you at least take a leave of absence from the shipping company?"

"No. I need the income."

"On the Diamond C you wouldn't need any money. I'll—"

"No!" Kaya managed to twist free of Joshua's hands. "I'll not live on anyone's charity. I never have and as long as there's breath in my body, I never will. Besides, you're the last person I'd accept help from."

"Okay, okay. If you want a job, you've got one on the Diamond C."

"What job?" she asked distrustfully. "Some busywork you're thinking up as we speak? No, thanks. I earn my money fair and square."

"No fake job. Remember my office?"

"Yes. It was a mess."

GET FREE BOOKS and a FREE GIFT WHEN YOU PLAY THE...

Lucky 7

Just scratch off the silver box with a coin. Then check below to see the gifts you get!

SLOT MACHINE GAME!

YES! I have scratched off the silver box. Please send me the 2 free Silhouette Romance® books and gift for which I qualify. I understand I am under no obligation to purchase any books, as explained on the back of this card.

310 SDL D72Q　　　　　　　　　　　　**210 SDL EEWJ**

FIRST NAME

LAST NAME

ADDRESS

APT.#

CITY

STATE/PROV.

ZIP/POSTAL CODE

7	7	7	**Worth TWO FREE BOOKS plus a BONUS Mystery Gift!**
🍒	🍒	🍒	**Worth TWO FREE BOOKS!**
♣	♣	♣	**Worth ONE FREE BOOK!**
🔔	🔔	🍒	**TRY AGAIN!**

www.eHarlequin.com

(S-R-02/06)

DETACH AND MAIL CARD TODAY!

The Silhouette Reader Service™ — Here's how it works:

Accepting your 2 free books and gift places you under no obligation to buy anything. You may keep the books and gift and return the shipping statement marked "cancel." If you do not cancel, about a month later we'll send you 4 additional books and bill you just $3.57 each in the U.S., or $4.05 each in Canada, plus 25¢ shipping & handling per book and applicable taxes if any.* That's the complete price and — compared to cover prices of $4.25 each in the U.S. and $4.99 each in Canada — it's quite a bargain! You may cancel at any time, but if you choose to continue, every month we'll send you 4 more books, which you may either purchase at the discount price or return to us and cancel your subscription.

*Terms and prices subject to change without notice. Sales tax applicable in N.Y. Canadian residents will be charged applicable provincial taxes and GST. Credit or debit balances in a customer's account(s) may be offset by any other outstanding balance owed by or to the customer.

"It still is. You could do the paperwork until my secretary comes back from maternity leave. I know you use a computer at work to track shipments. The spreadsheet I use isn't that different, I imagine. You could learn the program real fast." Kaya seemed to consider that carefully and Joshua breathed a little easier.

"How long before your secretary comes back?" she asked.

"Beginning of September. When Natalie goes back to school."

Kaya nodded. When she realized she was getting caught up in his scheme, she backpedaled fast. "No. I won't take Natalie to the Diamond C."

Joshua watched her remembering her deepest fear. "Nobody will say or do anything to Natalie. On the Diamond C or anywhere else," he said with absolute conviction.

"How can you be so sure of that? What if Lily suddenly came to the ranch and saw my daughter? What if she guessed that Natalie is her grandchild?"

"She won't come to the ranch. She never liked it that much. She only stayed because my father refused to live anywhere else. Besides, the ranch is mine."

Kaya was not reassured. "No. I can't risk Lily finding out. Even if she doesn't own the Diamond C, she might show up. Can't you imagine what that would be like? I won't expose Natalie to Lily's venom. No, we're staying right here."

"You think I'm no match for Lily?" Joshua asked incredulously.

"I don't know if you are or not, but I can't afford to take a chance on finding out. I will not allow my daughter to be called ugly names, to be made to feel second rate or less."

"I'm not my brother. Lily has no hold on me."

"We're not going."

"You don't understand, Kaya. You don't have a choice."

"What? What are you talking about?"

"I had hoped you'd see it my way and come to the ranch because it's best for you and Natalie. I'd hoped I wouldn't have to do this."

Kaya didn't like the ominous sound of this. An awful feeling of foreboding settled over her. "Do what?"

"Make you come to the ranch."

Even though she dreaded the answer, she had to ask. "How can you make me come?"

"There was a time limit on the account my father set up for you. It's run out."

Blindly Kaya reached out to locate the sofa. She sank onto it. "How can any one human being be this unlucky?" Kaya pressed her hands over her face.

Joshua sat down beside her. He drew her hands from her face to make her look at him. "Only good things will happen to you from now on. If you let me help you."

She gazed at him for a long time, her eyes searching his face for his true feelings.

Joshua sat motionless, knowing that the fate of three people hung in the balance.

Finally Kaya spoke. "You can help. Really help. You can pay that hospital bill and then leave us alone."

"That's the one thing I can't do. Natalie has a right to find out about her heritage. I know you despise us. And we Cunninghams," he added with a hint of apology in his voice, "have done things that weren't right, but so have you."

Kaya shook her head, ready to deny his claim.

"Yes, you have. You kept Natalie's existence a secret from her father's side of the family," Joshua reminded her. "And that was wrong."

Kaya closed her eyes. He was right. She'd had a good reason for not telling them about Natalie, but that didn't make it right.

"Why get somebody else to take care of Natalie while you work? At the ranch you could take care of her yourself. You can arrange your work hours to fit her schedule. It doesn't matter to me when you get the bookwork done."

Joshua watched her considering his offer. It was obvious that she liked the idea of being with her daughter all day long. He had her almost hooked. Casually he added, "My secretary receives a good salary, health insurance and the usual perks that go with such a job. And so would you. Doesn't that sound tempting?"

Kaya slanted him a long look. "You're as persuasive as Lucifer wooing a susceptible soul."

Joshua grinned. "I don't qualify for the role of Lucifer. Wasn't he the fairest of all the angels? I can hardly compete with him in the looks department."

"I wouldn't be so sure of that," Kaya muttered softly.

"Pardon?"

"Nothing."

"What do you say to my offer, Kaya?"

"Do I have a choice? You know I can't pay the hospital bill. And it'll be bigger by the time Natalie is released," she warned. The mere thought of that bill caused her to press the palms of her hands together to stop their shaking.

"It's not a bad deal I'm offering," Joshua pointed out.

"That remains to be seen. Part of me tells me that I'll regret this before long. Really regret it." Kaya felt a shiver of premonition.

"You won't regret it." Joshua wanted to take her hands

between his to reassure her, but he refrained. His touch might spook her into making the wrong decision.

She studied Joshua's face, wishing she could read his mind, his heart. But as he had said, she had no choice. For good or bad, she had to take his offer. "I'll have to ask my boss if he'll give me a couple of months off."

"He will."

"How can you be so sure of that?"

"Let's just say the man knows what's the politically and economically correct thing to do. Speak to him tomorrow. I want you and my niece at the ranch as soon as she's released from the hospital." Joshua headed for the door. Without turning, he said, "Good night, Kaya."

He was gone before she gathered her wits to speak.

Kaya pressed her hands against her temples where a headache pounded viciously. She had to talk to someone about this. Maria. Glancing at the clock, Kaya noted that it was past midnight. Too late to call.

She went into the bathroom to take three aspirin. Perhaps after a quick shower she could manage to get five hours of sleep. She was tired enough to sleep for a week, but her thoughts were in such turmoil that she might toss and turn all night long, wondering if the decision to move to the ranch even temporarily had been the right one.

Joshua was right about one thing. She couldn't work two jobs indefinitely on only five hours of sleep a night. Something had to give.

Over a quick breakfast of cereal and milk, Kaya wondered again if she should have refused Joshua's offer. And do what? Work until she collapsed to pay off even a fraction of her hospital debts? Then what? What would happen to Natalie if Kaya became seriously ill or had some sort of major breakdown? A series of foster homes? The prospect caused Kaya to shudder. Joshua had been right: she didn't really have a choice.

What was she so afraid of? Of that unexpected and un-explainable attraction she felt each time Joshua came into her field of vision? Kaya knew that was part of it. That and her unhappy history with the Cunningham family.

Loving and marrying Derrick had almost destroyed her. Hadn't she learned anything from that heartbreak? She had, but that bitter lesson didn't keep her knees from grow-ing weak, her heart from pounding, her pulse from leap-ing, her hands from trembling, every time Joshua came too close to her.

And when he touched her, kissed her…Kaya closed her eyes in agony. What was she going to do? Given her idi-otic reaction to the man, how could she live with him in the same house?

With great difficulty and extreme vigilance.

She'd have to watch her every move, her every word, her every glance. And stay out of his way. On a place as big as the Diamond C, that shouldn't be too difficult. That was the answer: avoid Joshua Cunningham like the plague because to her he was as dangerous as the plague. She could do that. Still, she needed to talk to someone. Her cousin. First, she had to speak with her boss.

Her boss promised Kaya that she could have her job back in September. For the summer he could hire a college student to take her place.

At noon Kaya met Maria at Jack's Diner. Over ham-burgers and fries they discussed the latest development.

"Seems to me Joshua Cunningham is acting very honorably, helping you and Natalie this way. Very responsible. I don't think you'll have to worry about him trying to take Natalie away from you. What judge in his right mind would give custody of a little girl to a bachelor? And your former mother-in-law? Well, since she doesn't come to the ranch, she's no threat. Even if she comes, an occasional exposure to Lily won't harm Natalie."

"I wish I could be sure of that."

"You've been a good mother. Raised Natalie right. Lily can't undo that. It's too late. Natalie's character is formed. She's a strong little girl. She's got the right values. She's got self-confidence."

"I've tried to be a good mother," Kaya said softly.

"You are a good mother. Quit worrying." Eyeing Kaya's untouched food, she asked, "So what else is bothering you about going to live on the Diamond C?"

Kaya shrugged but avoided looking into Maria's eyes.

"Your boss promised to give you your job back when you're ready to return. You'll be taken care of at the ranch..." Maria backtracked. "Is that what's bothering you? Being take care of? Shoot, Kaya. You've taken care of yourself since junior high and a baby as well since you were eighteen. Relax. Let someone else do it for a change."

"I'm so tired that right now this sounds tempting," Kaya admitted.

"Consider it a vacation. Lord knows you've never taken one. You've been working so hard, you deserve to take it a little easier. You're not Superwoman."

"I know that."

Maria quietly watched her cousin. Finally she said, "But being taken care of is not what's worrying you."

"No."

"Is it Joshua Cunningham?"

"Yes. There's this thing between us. This attraction." Kaya broke off, shrugging in helpless confusion.

"There've been attractions between men and women since the beginning of time," Maria pointed out. "The man and the woman either do something about it or they don't."

"I don't want to do anything about it."

"Then don't."

"It isn't that simple."

"Ah. The attraction is that strong. You're afraid you might not be tough enough to fight it successfully?"

Kaya nodded.

"Would it be so awful if you had a man in your life? You've been alone a long time. And you've known Joshua, you—"

"No! He and I... No." Kaya shook her head vigorously. "No, no. Being involved with Joshua would be as disastrous as my marriage was." Kaya shivered.

"How can you be so sure? Is he that much like his younger brother?"

"Joshua's not anything like Derrick."

"So what's the problem?"

"He's still a Cunningham and I'm still...who I am. But there's more. Joshua blames me for Derrick's death."

Maria looked shocked. "But how can he? You weren't even there. Derrick let you go. It isn't fair of Joshua to blame you. Are you sure he does?"

"Pretty sure. We've never talked it out, so I don't know everything he holds against me, but it's plenty, believe me."

"Maybe you should have it out with him once and for all."

Kaya drew a shuddering breath. "I agree with you, but it'll be hard with Natalie there. We should have settled this before now. You know she senses it when something's wrong."

Maria nodded. "The kid's got built-in radar. But don't you think she'll notice the strain between you and Joshua if you don't clear the air?"

"Probably. Another no-win situation," Kaya murmured. "But you're right. As much as I dread this confrontation, we've got to get it over with."

Maria touched her cousin's hand reassuringly before she spoke. "If this arrangement on the ranch doesn't work out, you can always come and stay with us," she offered.

"That wouldn't do at all." Remembering what Joshua had said about Manny, Kaya shook her head ruefully.

"What? Tell me," Maria insisted.

"Joshua's investigator saw me deliver the groceries to your place. Joshua thought Manny was my young stud."

"What?" Maria exclaimed. "And I bet Joshua didn't like the idea of you having a young stud. Wait till I tell Manny he's a stud. On second thought, I'd better not. He'd be impossible to live with."

"Anyway, I'm keeping the apartment. I know it would be smarter to try to sublet it for the summer and save the rent money, but I need the security of it being there. It's our home."

"I understand. You know I'll keep Natalie if you decide to come back before school starts."

"Thanks."

The two women smiled at each other with affection.

"How much farther, Mommy?"

"Not much. We're getting closer."

"Can I sit up?" Natalie asked as she fiddled with the seat belt her mother had fastened over her.

"As soon as we reach the boundary line of the Diamond C." Kaya looked into the rearview mirror at her daughter. She'd made a bed for Natalie on the back seat, but ever since the little girl had awakened from her nap, she'd been pleading to be allowed to sit up and look out the window.

A couple of miles down the road, Kaya said, "Look, the big gateposts are coming into view."

"Wow. Is that the sign of the ranch hanging from the post?" Natalie asked, craning her neck for a better look.

"Yes. That's the Diamond C brand. How do you feel?"

"Fine. I can't wait to see the horses and the cows, and Joshua said he'd teach me to ride and—"

"Whoa. Not so fast. Remember what Dr. Reiger said?"

The excitement on Natalie's face died. Kaya felt guilty for destroying her daughter's joy. Gently she added, "He didn't say you had to stay in bed all day, remember? You can do those things but you have to work up to them. Do some each day until you're strong. By the end of the summer you'll have done them all." Kaya crossed her fingers surreptitiously and offered a quick, silent prayer of supplication for her words to become reality.

"Mommy, look. Cowboys. And they're waving," Natalie said, returning the wave shyly but smilingly.

Kaya acknowledged the men's salute, wondering what, if anything, Joshua had told the ranch hands about his houseguests. Most likely it would have been Clancy who'd informed them of their arrival. Had Natalie's identity been revealed? Joshua hadn't told her anything, only that he expected her on Saturday.

When she'd picked up Natalie, the business office had

handed her a receipt marked Paid In Full. Kaya had felt as if a truckload of rocks had been removed from her back. Now she wondered if the unease squeezing her chest as she pulled up to the ranch house was really such an improvement over the rocks. Maybe she had merely traded in one set of worries for another. Then she chided herself. Joshua was right. She anticipated worries and troubles that often didn't even happen. .

Joshua came out to meet them. He must have been watching from the window of his office to arrive outside as quickly as he did. He wore jeans that seemed to have been made to order to his long legs and lean hips, boots with heels that added height he didn't need and emphasized that sexy, swivel-hipped gait she didn't need to notice if she wanted to retain her hold on logic and aloofness. He'd rolled up the sleeves of the blue-checked cotton shirt he wore, exposing muscular arms covered with pale blond hair.

He looked every inch a male in his prime. Sexy. Seductive. Dangerous. Kaya felt her mouth go dry and her palms dampen up. Not a good start. Not after the serious talking to she'd given herself all the way to the ranch about staying cool and unimpressed and unaffected by the man.

"Did you have a good trip?"

Joshua had asked the question as if the answer really mattered to him. If he really cared, he wouldn't have forced her to make the trip in the first place. He was being polite for Natalie's sake. Knowing that her daughter was watching, Kaya forced herself to smile.

"The trip was fine." Shooting him a sidelong look, she added, "I half expected you to come and escort us back to the ranch."

"I was going to give you another thirty minutes before starting for town and providing escort services," he said, half teasingly. Then he turned to Natalie. "And how are you?"

"Fine. I slept most of the way, so I'm all slept out," Natalie said with a look at her mother.

"She's trying to get out of her afternoon rest," Kaya explained to Joshua. Looking at her daughter indulgently, she added, "I think for today you can skip your nap."

Natalie grinned happily. "Can I look at the horses?" Natalie asked Joshua, her blue eyes dancing with excitement.

"After a while. Clancy baked cookies especially for you. It would hurt his feelings if we didn't go in to sample them. Is that okay?"

When Natalie nodded, Joshua picked up the two large suitcases, while Kaya carried her overnight case and Natalie's bedding.

For an instant she paused on the porch, remembering her wedding day and her arrival on the Diamond C for the very first time. Except then she hadn't walked up the steps. She'd floated up on the wings of newly-wed bliss, love and the naive expectation of a happy forever-after. So much for youthful idealism and romantic dreams. She felt a tiny stab of regret tug at her heart for that lost belief in dreams of romance and love everlasting.

Clancy hovered in the doorway of the kitchen. "Baked you some cookies," Clancy said to Natalie, never taking his eyes off the little girl.

Sniffing the fragrant air, she asked, her voice hopeful, "Chocolate chip?"

"Is there any other kind?" Clancy asked.

As they sat at the table, Joshua couldn't stop looking at Natalie, either.

"So, did you bring the list of foods the doctor wants you to eat?" Clancy asked the little girl.

Natalie wrinkled her small nose. "Stuff with iron in it, like liver. Yuck."

"Well, there's other stuff on the list, I'm sure, so we won't have to eat liver often," he said consolingly. "I remember your daddy eatin' a lot of good Diamond C beef when he was sick. We'll make out just fine," he added.

"You knew my daddy?" Natalie asked, her voice reverent.

"Sure did. All his life."

"Will you tell me all about him?"

Clancy looked at Kaya, his eyes seeking her reaction. When she nodded slightly, he said, "We've got all summer to talk about your daddy."

Natalie smiled at Clancy. Kaya thought the old cowboy's eyes looked suspiciously bright, as if misted by happy tears.

When Natalie excused herself to go to the bathroom, the three adults sat silently for a moment. Then Clancy spoke.

"If you put a blond wig on that child she could pass for Derrick's twin sister at the same age. It's amazin'."

"Really?" Kaya asked.

Joshua nodded. "I saw her being wheeled down the hall at the hospital and I knew who she was without having to ask anybody."

"I guess I'm so used to seeing her every day that I never realized how strong the resemblance was." Kaya stared into her coffee cup, her forehead wrinkled in a frown.

"What's the matter?" Joshua asked.

Natalie returned, preventing Kaya from responding.

Joshua carried their bags upstairs. Kaya took the porch room again, while Natalie exclaimed happily over the room with the Western motif that adjoined her mother's. Too impatient to wait for her mother to finish unpacking, Natalie begged to go outside to look at the corral. Clancy was only too happy to take her.

Joshua sat on the bed, watching Kaya place clothes into Natalie's chest of drawers. She wore tailored khaki shorts and an emerald T-shirt that intensified the green color of her eyes. The shorts displayed her long legs which caused him to swallow a couple of times.

Gaining control of his voice, he said, "I wasn't sure you'd come."

"I wasn't sure, either, but you didn't give me much choice."

"You could have run."

"Yes. I thought about it. And go how far before your private detective found me?"

"Not very far," he admitted without shame and with just a trace of smugness.

"That's what I thought."

Joshua watched her firm, shapely bottom as she bent to place T-shirts into a lower drawer. He forced himself to lean back on his elbows, placing his hands out of temptation's way.

Without turning, Kaya said, "Natalie sure is excited about the ranch. I'm going to have my hands full, getting her to take her naps." She straightened up and stepped back.

She was close enough that he smelled the scent she wore, something subtle, slightly sweet with just a suggestion of a tart, sharp undertone, like an exotic rainforest blossom that might possess magic powers—or deadly ones. The scent struck his senses forcefully, alluringly.

She turned suddenly and caught him staring at her like

a thirsty man lost in the desert stares at a mirage of a clean, sweet water hole.

Her green eyes widened slightly. Her dusky skin became suffused with warm color. She'd recognized his purely male appreciation of her. How could she have missed it, he thought bitterly, when he'd allowed his guard to slip. For the first time he seriously wondered if perhaps he'd made the biggest mistake of his life by asking her to come to the Diamond C. He'd been so caught up in helping his niece that he'd overlooked the hazard her mother presented.

"What?" Kaya asked to break the long silence and the intense eye contact.

"I was wondering why you frowned so when Clancy and I commented on how much Natalie looked like her father. Do you hate Derrick so much that it bothers you that his daughter favors him?"

"Of course not. I don't hate Derrick. Where did you get that dumb idea?"

"From a few things you've said. Oh, you didn't use the word hate, but disappointment, and falling short, and terms like that which aren't that far removed from hate."

"I frowned because if you and Clancy had no trouble seeing Natalie's resemblance to Derrick, then Lily's bound to see it, too. And that scares the living daylights out of me."

"I told you. Lily won't show up here. Not during the hot, dusty summer months which she claims are too hard on her delicate complexion." Joshua uncurled himself from the bed. A couple of steps brought him to her. Gently he placed his hands on her upper arms. "Don't worry about my stepmother. I'll take care of her should she show up. Which she won't."

She looked at him probingly, lengthily with her express-

ive green eyes. That gaze cut all the way to his bone mar-
row. Without a conscious act of will his hands unwound
the scarf from her head and tangled in her thick, coarse-
silk hair. How he enjoyed the feel of Kaya's hair between
his fingers. How he loved her scent. How he longed to taste
her lips. He must have urged her closer, for suddenly his
eyes were filled only with her lovely face.

"Kaya," he whispered against her lips. When she didn't
pull back, the temptation to press his lips against hers
drove out all thoughts of resistance and recriminations.
She was the woman he desired as he had desired no other,
and she was in his arms. He would have to have been made
of stone to let her go. The kiss started out hot and heady.
Passion leaped in him high, like a flame fed by a blast of
pure oxygen. Joshua felt nothing but a pleasure so intense
it bordered on exquisite pain. He wanted the exquisite pain
to go on forever.

"No!" With a burst of strength she didn't know she had,
Kaya wedged her hands against Joshua's chest. "That's one
of the reasons I didn't want to come to the ranch. This can't
be happening between us. It absolutely can't."

Joshua blinked to clear his sensation-laden brain. "I
agree it isn't the smartest thing for us to get involved, but
I wouldn't put it as strongly as an absolute impossibility."

"Oh, you wouldn't?"

"No. We're strongly attracted to each other, we're both
single, we are not related by blood, years have passed
since—"

"Stop right there. You keep hinting at all sorts of awful
things I'm supposed to have done to Derrick, but still you'd
kiss me and make love to me?" Kaya shook her head.

She pulled free and backed away from Joshua. She

glanced out the window. Clancy and Natalie were standing by the corral, looking at the horses. It didn't appear as if they'd be on their way back to the house soon.

Confrontation time. Kaya couldn't put if off any longer. Taking a deep breath, she turned back to Joshua.

"This is as good a time as any. Let's have this out once and for all. What exactly is it that you accuse me of? And don't hold back." Kaya faced Joshua, her face pale but her head held high.

Chapter Seven

"You sure you want to do this?" Joshua asked.

"No, I don't want to do this," Kaya replied with a sigh. "I'd have to have a self-destructive streak a mile wide in me if I really wanted to engage in the kind of emotional bloodletting this is probably going to degenerate into."

"We don't have to do this."

"Yes, we do. If we're going to live in the same house for the next two months, we have to clear the air. I could probably cope with your verbal digs and thinly veiled references to the sins you think I'm guilty of, but Natalie can't. She needs to get her strength back, not worry why you and I are at odds. She's a sensitive child. She'd notice that kind of tension between us, and it would upset her."

Kaya waited for Joshua to speak. She hadn't lied when she'd said she didn't want to have this argument with him. She'd much rather go back to what they'd been doing a few seconds before. She loved the way he kissed her, the way he held her, the way he molded her against him until their bodies fit the way nature intended them to fit.

Startled, Kaya wondered how and when these dangerous feelings had taken root. What was the matter with her?

Had she lost her mind? Why was she indulging in day-dreams about something that could never be? Perhaps if she were a childless woman she could abandon herself to such pleasures. But she was the mother of a small girl just getting over a serious illness whose recovery couldn't be endangered by anything—least of all her mother's selfish indulgences. Especially if these indulgences involved a man she didn't entirely trust.

Joshua had said he would keep Lily away from Natalie. What if he changed his mind? She looked at him and saw that he was watching her intently.

"Well, why don't you start? I had the distinct impression that you could hardly wait to get at me. Here's your chance." Kaya threw her arms wide open in a gesture that left her body, her heart, defenseless. She couldn't understand why Joshua hesitated, couldn't understand that strange expression in his bright blue eyes.

"All right," Joshua finally said. "If Derrick hadn't been killed, would you have told him about the baby?"

"Yes," Kaya replied without hesitation. "I grew up without knowing my father. I wouldn't have prevented my child from knowing hers. I would never have done that to Natalie." She looked at him curiously. "You grew up with only one parent. Wouldn't you have preferred to have both?"

Joshua dismissed her question with an impatient gesture. "We're not talking about me. You didn't tell her about her father's side of the family. Why not? She must have asked. It would have been natural for her to want to know."

"I always thought that I'd tell her when she was grown up. When her character had been completely formed. When she was independent and old enough to form her own judgments." Kaya winced when she realized how self-righteous and condemning her words sounded. Judging by the tight white line around his mouth, she knew her words had stung Joshua.

"What were we? The original family from hell?" he demanded, his voice edged with the temper he was trying to control. "Did you think our influence would have been that awful on the child?"

"Lily's would have been. I know," Kaya said, pressing the palms of her hands together, "that I'm not objective where my former mother-in-law is concerned. Possibly she has some good qualities, but I never saw them. I truly believe that she's a dreadful, cruel human being. I don't want her anywhere near my daughter. Or me. That's how I feel. I can't help it."

"You're entitled to your feelings."

He'd said that in a strangely quiet, almost gentle voice. And he didn't defend Lily. That was a good sign and it made Kaya feel hopeful.

"So you decided to tough it out alone. I can understand that, I think. What I can't understand is your original decision to leave. To give up on your marriage. Your husband. You weren't here to see what that did to Derrick. You didn't have to watch him start to self-destruct. You abandoned him, and by doing that, you condemned him to death."

"No!" Kaya cried out, her hopeful feelings dashed. "My leaving was meant to do the opposite. I left to save him. To save our marriage."

"Double-talk, Kaya. You don't abandon someone in order to save them." He shook his head impatiently. "That makes no sense."

"Try to understand. Please, for once, try to listen to me with an open mind," she pleaded, her eyes bright with tears.

"All right," Joshua said. "Go ahead. Explain." He stood with his legs firmly planted and his arms crossed over his chest. His lips were pressed together in an uncompromising line, emphasizing the small scar above his upper lip.

Kaya almost gave up in despair right then and there. Didn't Joshua realize that his stance, his body language, betrayed his reluctance to listen objectively? Kaya swallowed to ease the pain of unshed tears in her throat. Though it was tempting to throw in the towel, she owed it to Natalie to try to make her uncle understand the past. Taking a shuddering breath, she began again.

"Some of what happened was my fault. I know that. I admit that. I came to this house as a foolish young girl, but being young isn't a valid excuse. I should have known what to expect, but because Derrick loved me and made me his wife, I thought, I hoped, I'd be accepted. Maybe I chose to forget the lessons in prejudice that all the preceding years of my life had taught me because I was so much in love. Because love changed the way the world looked to me. I thought maybe the world would look at me differently, too. Dumb, huh?" she asked with a bitter smile.

"Seems to me the expectation to be accepted by the family of the person you married wasn't dumb or unreasonable," Joshua conceded.

"In most places, maybe, but not on the Diamond C."

"You're confusing the Diamond C with Lily. They're not the same. Not by a long shot."

"Maybe not, but to me at that time they were the same. Lily ruled this house and everyone in it. Especially Derrick and me."

"Okay, I can see that life here wasn't easy for you, but

did you really give it a chance? It appears to me you left awfully easy and awfully fast."

"Because Derrick was beginning to change, and I knew if I stayed, he'd stop loving me." Looking at Joshua earnestly, imploringly, she tried to convince him to see her side of the past. "You see, if someone is told something often enough, he'll eventually believe it. Lily took every chance she got to strip me verbally of every good quality I ever possessed. She kept telling Derrick over and over that I was nothing but poor trash, out for only one thing: his family's money."

Kaya closed her eyes, the pain of the memory sharp and bitter. "I could see him begin to wonder if marrying me, loving me, was a mistake. His mother had such a powerful hold on him that I thought the only chance for us to make it was to leave here. That's how it seemed to me at the time. Maybe I was wrong."

"Maybe you were," Joshua agreed, his voice grave. Kaya looked at him, her inner torment visible on her face.

"Don't you think I've thought about that? Second-guessed my decision to leave a million times? I wasn't sure I was doing the right thing when I walked out the front door of this house. Part of me hoped Derrick would stop me. But he didn't. Even while I waited for the bus at the Crossroads I almost turned around and hitched a ride back to the ranch, thinking that if I tried one more time to convince him, I might succeed."

"Convince him of what?" Joshua asked.

"To go away with me. To start a life together, just him and me. Find a room somewhere, get jobs. I knew it wouldn't be easy for him because he'd never been poor, had never lacked for anything, but I believed with me by his side, loving him with all my heart, he could make it."

"Make it doing what? Pumping gas? Bagging groceries? Waiting tables?"

Kaya turned on Joshua, every inch of her body seething with righteous anger. "And why not? There's nothing wrong with any of those jobs. I've earned my living doing some of them. They didn't degrade—"

"Don't jump all over me, Kaya. I didn't say there was anything wrong with them—for most people, me included. But Derrick?" Joshua shook his head emphatically. "He'd never done much of any kind of work."

"I know, but that wasn't my fault."

"I didn't say it was. Don't assume, Kaya, and calm down."

"I am calm." Realizing that she wasn't, she took a deep breath. "I didn't suggest that he'd have to get that kind of work. He had only one year of college left. He could have gotten work that paid better, in an office maybe. He could have finished his degree. I don't believe Ray would have refused to pay Derrick's tuition, but even if he had, we could still have managed. It would have taken longer, but that's all."

"You had it all planned out. You were dead sure of everything."

She shook her head. "No, I didn't have it all planned, but I hoped that away from the Diamond C our marriage would work. And the only thing I was dead sure of was that Derrick and I didn't have a chance as long as we stayed at the ranch. I'm still convinced of that."

She walked to the window. She rested her forehead against the smooth glass and closed her eyes. She wanted to stop talking, to stop remembering and reliving the painful past, but having come this far, she decided to finish. Kaya doubted she had the strength to go through this ordeal again.

"I gave Derrick Maria's address. I told him she would know where I was if he changed his mind. Like a lovesick fool I prayed he'd come after me. I still hoped he'd do that, even after he let me walk out of this house. I hoped for that, I prayed for that, every single day until the night I heard of his death." Kaya's eyes filled with tears, recalling that shattering moment.

"Derrick wasn't strong enough to leave the ranch, and I wasn't strong enough to stay," she murmured, her voice filled with sadness. "That was our misfortune."

Joshua stared at Kaya for several seconds. Then he shrugged. "Well, that's your version. I remember things a little differently. When Derrick discovered you'd gone, he trashed the room you'd shared with him. Really trashed it. I kept him from ripping the big fan out of the ceiling, but that was pretty much the only thing that was left intact. He was bitter and angry. What man wouldn't be when his wife walks out on him? That's the kind of betrayal nobody ever forgets."

"But that's not—" Kaya stopped, knowing that she couldn't make Joshua see how it had been for her. She wasn't clever or eloquent enough for that. With a weary shake of her head she resumed unpacking. She arranged Natalie's books on the shelf. The tense silence lengthened into minutes before Joshua broke it.

"After you left, Derrick went a little crazy. Drank too much. Chased too… Um, chased all over the county in a fast Ferrari Lily bought him."

"A fancy, expensive Italian car in exchange for an unsuitable wife? Not a bad trade," Kaya said, her voice ringing with irony. A mirthless smile curled around her lips.

"It wasn't like that," Joshua said quickly. "Derrick didn't

ask for the car. He was really surprised when it arrived one morning. But that's beside the point. The point is, he didn't seem to give a damn about anything, including his own safety and survival."

Hearing the accusation in Joshua's tone, Kaya said, "He knew where I was. He could have come to me at any time."

"He shouldn't have had to come after you. You were his wife. You should have been with him!" Joshua saw the flare of temper in Kaya's eyes. He also saw her clamp her jaws together in an effort to control it. When she spoke, her voice was more ironic and hurt than angry.

Taking a deep breath, she asked, "Haven't you heard anything I've said?"

"Every word. Your version. Your side of the story."

Kaya's shoulders slumped in weariness. Then a wave of anger infused her with new energy. "Don't you dare blame this on a *misunderstanding* that could be solved with a few words. Don't you dare do that to me. You told me that you heard our voices through the wall. We talked. I talked until I was hoarse. Derrick understood what I was saying. He just couldn't leave the ranch and take a chance on us, and I couldn't stay." Kaya paused to take a calming breath.

"You understand what I'm talking about. Or you could, but then you would have to admit that what happened to Derrick wasn't all my fault. The rest of you would have to accept some responsibility for his destructive streak, including you, his big brother, and you're not ready to do that. So much easier to blame it all on the faithless wife who deserted him. But I have news for you. It's not all my fault, and the sooner you accept that, the sooner we'll get along a whole lot better."

She watched Joshua's face. It was a mixture of denial

and outrage. "If you're fair, Joshua, you'll look at the past from all angles, not just from your own narrow perspective. There are two sides to almost everything."

"I'm back, Mommy," Natalie said, standing in the doorway, her eyes flicking uncertainly back and forth between the adults.

"Hi, sweetie," Kaya said with a smile meant to reassure the little girl who seemed to sense the tension in the room. "I was just unpacking your books." Seeing the book in Kaya's hand, Natalie ran to her mother and took it.

"You read this book to me, Uncle Joshua. Remember?"

"Yeah, I remember. In the hospital, the day we met."

"Will you read it to me again?"

"I will. Some other time, pumpkin. Right now I've got to see to some things on the ranch." Joshua touched Natalie's hair and even managed to smile at the little girl before he left.

Natalie plopped down on the bed.

"Tell me about the horses," Kaya said to her daughter, watching the tall man leave the room, knowing she had failed to explain to him what it had been like for her all those years ago. And having failed, she knew that her relationship with Joshua would be filled with tension and problems.

Relationship? That was an odd word to use to describe the boss-secretary, host-houseguest roles they'd been thrown into for the summer. Had she subconsciously chosen the word because what she really longed to have with Joshua was a personal relationship? An intimate male-female kind of relationship? Dear heaven above, was the chemistry between them so strong that it was inevitably leading to deeper feelings? That's all she needed to complicate her life: falling for Joshua Cunningham.

She wouldn't, couldn't, allow herself to develop any kind of romantic feelings for Joshua. Having been burned once, had taught her how dangerous the fires of love were. She simply had to keep her distance and her guardedness. Love? How had that word crept into her thoughts? A mistake. A temporary aberration. She couldn't possibly use that word in connection with Joshua. She was neither stupid nor insane.

"Mommy, which color of a horse do you like better?"

"Pardon?" Kaya realized she'd stopped listening to her daughter some minutes ago.

"Oh, Mommy!" Natalie said, her voice imbued by the considerable impatience an almost five-year-old was capable of. "Which do you think is prettier? A brown horse or a yellow horse?" she repeated.

"Sorry, I was thinking of something else, but I think both are beautiful."

"But if you had to choose?"

"The yellow." Dismayed, Kaya wondered if she'd chosen that color because Joshua rode a palomino stallion. Probably. That sort of seemingly innocent preoccupation with Joshua would never do. She'd have to control her thoughts and feelings much more diligently.

Natalie sighed. "I can't make up my mind."

"Why do you have to make up your mind?"

"Because Clancy said that Uncle Joshua picked out two horses I could learn to ride on."

"Let me guess. A roan and a palomino, right?"

"Uh-huh."

"Well, you don't have to decide this minute, do you?"

"No."

"Good. Then just think about it for a while." Kaya observed her daughter. Natalie looked a little tired, but having promised that she didn't have to take an afternoon nap, Kaya knew better than to suggest that. Still, she had to find some way to get Natalie to rest. In a very casual tone, Kaya said, "Why don't you sit in that nice rocking chair over by the window and look at a picture book for a while?"

"Okay."

Natalie selected a book and settled down in the rocker, leaving Kaya free to pursue her speculations about her worrisome attraction to Joshua.

Despite the rocky beginning, Kaya had settled into a smooth routine at the ranch. At least it was smooth when Joshua wasn't around. The moment he came near her, all her nerve ends jumped into the alert mode.

Kaya turned the computer off and walked down to the corral where Clancy was giving Natalie a riding lesson. Kaya leaned against the corral, never taking her eyes off of her daughter.

"You can loosen your death grip on the rail," Joshua said, joining Kaya. "Clancy knows what he's doing. He put me on my first horse. Derrick, too. Relax." Casually he placed his hand over hers.

"I know Clancy is careful. It's just that the horses seem so big and Natalie is so small."

"Nifty's as docile and gentle a horse as you could wish for. Besides, she's way past her galloping and bucking years. If she ever had any. Not bucking years, anyway." He was talking, he realized, merely to put Kaya at ease, not to make brilliant conversation. Ever since their discussion on the day of her arrival, she had been distant. He had the distinct impression that she was trying to avoid him. Joshua had cut her some slack since he had needed some time for himself as well.

He had tried to forget what she had said about Derrick and his family, but he hadn't succeeded. Her words haunted him. Occasionally he even suspected that more than a little of what she'd said might be true. He didn't like that one bit.

Even though he admitted that it was probably smarter if they continued to stay away from each other, he found it more and more difficult to do that. Whenever he heard Kaya's voice in a room, he felt himself drawn toward that room as if by a magnet. She was like an itch he couldn't scratch. He ached to scratch it and see what that felt like, where that would lead them.

What was the worst thing that could happen if he continued to seek out her company? Joshua considered that for a while. He concluded that the natural course of events as he could see it at the moment was that they would part at the end of the summer, and that he would miss her. He was going to miss Kaya anyway, even if nothing more passed between them.

She'd been back on the ranch for three weeks. *Three weeks*. Yet in that short time she and Natalie had added more life and warmth to the old place than it had known in years. He hadn't been aware of the silence and the solitude that had hung over the house. Or that something had been missing from his life. Whenever he'd felt vaguely dissatisfied in the past, he'd added another project to his schedule. He'd filled his life with work.

Kaya hadn't moved her hand from beneath his. This sign of trust pleased him. She was bareheaded. In the bright sun, her hair glistened like a raven's wing. As she leaned forward, her white tank top gaped slightly, revealing the line where her light tan ended, just above the swell of her lovely breasts. He pictured the tips of his fingers tracing this tan line, slipping under the lacy edge of her bra, touching the satiny softness beneath. Heat raced to his belly. A slight dizziness fogged his brain.

"Oh, no!"

Kaya's whispered exclamation brought him back to reality. Taking in the scene before him, he saw what had alarmed her to the extent that she'd grasped his arm with her free hand.

"It's okay," he assured her. "Nifty likes being hugged." Natalie, her riding lesson over, had thrown her arms around the horse's lowered head. "Natalie's a natural rider. Must be in the genes," Joshua added.

"The Cunningham half of her genes. Not mine," Kaya said.

"You did okay on a horse as I remember. We'll go for a ride soon." Kaya looked at him, her green eyes wide and startled. He loved gazing into their intriguing depths.

"But it's been years since I've been on a horse!" she protested.

Kaya withdrew her hand from under his. Joshua regretted that. "Riding a horse is like riding a bicycle. You don't forget. It'll come back to you. Be ready at seven." He turned away to open the corral door.

"You did real good," he told Natalie, who beamed at him with shy pleasure. "You'll be a first-rate rider by the end of the summer." Taking Natalie's hand, they started toward the house.

Kaya followed slowly, trying to assimilate the various signals Joshua had sent her.

She supervised Natalie's bath and settled her in bed. Joshua arrived in time to read her a story as he had promised.

"I brought you something your mom thought you'd like," Joshua said, handing Natalie a paper bag.

"A present?" Natalie asked eagerly.

"Sort of."

Natalie removed what looked like a picture frame. Kaya's breath caught in her throat.

"It's a photo of your daddy," Joshua said.

Natalie studied the picture intently. Even though Kaya couldn't see it, she knew it was the portrait Joshua had found in the file cabinet on her first trip to the ranch.

"My daddy was handsome, wasn't he?" Natalie asked.

"He was," Joshua and Kaya said at the same time.

"I'll keep this picture on my nightstand from now on," Natalie announced. After she'd moved it around until she'd found the right spot for it, she said, "Thank you, Uncle Joshua." Impulsively she threw her arms around Joshua's neck for a tight hug. "I hope you like hugs as much as Nifty does."

"I do," Joshua said with a warm grin.

Over the child's head, Kaya caught Joshua's glance. "Thank you," she mouthed.

After reading the story to Natalie, Joshua walked down the stairs with Kaya.

"That was a lovely gesture," Kaya said, "giving Natalie that photo of Derrick. I have only a couple of snapshots of him. When I asked you for it that day, I wanted it for her."

"That's what I figured."

Downstairs they parted. Kaya went into the office to work, Joshua to the bunkhouse to discuss the next day's work with the men.

About an hour later, Joshua joined her, carrying a tray. He set it down on the filing cabinet.

"Can you shut that thing off?" Joshua asked, indicating

the computer. "Clancy's convinced you must be starving by now," Joshua said.

Looking at the slice of lemon-coconut cake Joshua handed her, Kaya felt her mouth water. "I'm hardly starving, not after that dinner I ate earlier, but this cake looks good. If I'm not careful, I'll have to go on a diet soon," she said, placing the first forkful of cake into her mouth. She savored it before she spoke. "Oh, this is so good."

They ate in silence. When they had finished, Joshua took the plate from her hand. He placed the dishes on the tray.

"There's a tiny piece of coconut stuck in the corner of your mouth," Joshua murmured.

Before Kaya could react, he'd reached out to remove it. His finger lingered on the corner of her mouth for a moment before he traced the outline of her lips. He continued to do so until her mouth tingled from his touch. Though she knew her voice would sound weak, Kaya felt compelled to ask, "Are you trying to memorize the shape of my mouth?"

"Uh-huh. Memorize it with my eyes, my fingertips, my lips. I'm going to kiss you, okay?" he asked, his velvet voice hardly more than a whisper.

"You're actually asking my permission?" Kaya moved her head back far enough to escape that erotic touch of his fingers on her mouth.

"Do I normally just grab you whether you want to be kissed or not?"

"No. You usually give me time to pull away, to refuse," she conceded softly.

"Are you going to pull away?" he asked, his eyes never leaving hers.

"I ought to. I really should, but I probably won't," she admitted unhappily.

"Should. Ought. Terrible words," Joshua murmured. "Not that there isn't a place and a time for them, but this isn't it."

His blue-eyed gaze mesmerized her. She felt deprived of free will, of choice, of the ability to think clearly, rationally, though Joshua hadn't even touched her yet. Except her lips, which still tingled. When he did, the palm of one of his hands cupping her nape while the other curled around a fist-ful of hair, Kaya felt a tremor rise from deep within her.

Joshua kissed her gently, carefully. At least in the beginning. But the longer their lips touched, the stronger the currents leaped and sparked between them. As the hunger grew, so did the intensity of their kisses. Kaya was vaguely aware that Joshua pulled her out of her chair and into his lap. Without thinking her arms encircled his neck and her fingers caressed his hair. It wasn't until his hand cupped her bare breast that reality broke through her emotion-numbed brain.

"Joshua." Kaya removed his hand with a sigh. "We have to stop."

"Why?"

"Because this is much too dangerous. We have a long, hot Texas summer ahead of us. If we don't stop this kissing and touching, you know where this will lead."

"Where?"

"With you in my bed or I in yours," Kaya said bluntly, adjusting her clothes, "and Natalie just down the hall. I can't risk that."

"Risk that? I don't understand the risk you're talking about. You know I wouldn't hurt you."

Kaya slid out of his arms. She backed several steps away. "If we became lovers, how do you think that would look to a judge should there ever be a custody hearing? Shacking up with my own brother-in-law in his house in a room next to my daughter's?" Kaya shivered, picturing herself in front of a stern, disapproving judge.

In a smooth, swift movement, Joshua rose from his chair. He loomed over Kaya. "How many times do I have to tell you that neither I nor anyone else will take Natalie away from you? Why don't you trust me?"

"How many times do I have to tell you that I didn't abandon Derrick the way you think I did? Why don't you believe me?"

They faced each other. Though their lips still burned from the kisses they'd shared, the chasm between them still seemed unbridgeable.

Kaya felt unspeakable sadness take possession of her. It pressed on her heart like physical pain.

"Good night, Joshua," Kaya murmured, her voice liquid with tears. She ran from the room.

Chapter Eight

Two days later Natalie was crabby. Nothing suited her. That was unusual behavior for her. Kaya studied her daughter intently.

"Come here, please." When Natalie came to stand next to her mother's chair, Kaya slid her hand between her daughter's shoulder blades. The skin was warm. Too warm. Kaya felt the first waves of anxiety sweep over her. *Be calm,* she told herself.

"I think we better take your temperature," Kaya said, grateful that her voice didn't reveal her anxiety.

"Oh, Mommy," Natalie wailed. "I'm fine."

"Probably, but we have to make sure." She saw Natalie swallow painfully. "Your throat's sore, isn't it?"

"A little."

Using a teaspoon as a tongue depressor, she saw what she'd been afraid of: Natalie's throat was a fiery-red. When she took the reading on the thermometer, she knew they were in trouble and so did Natalie. The little girl couldn't hide the fear that flickered briefly in her eyes before she put on her brave mask.

"I don't want to go to the hospital again," Natalie said, her voice small.

"I know, sweetie, and maybe you won't have to. I'll call the doctor."

"I'll bet I have to go."

Kaya didn't have the heart to offer false hope.

While Kaya was on the telephone with Dr. Reiger, Joshua came into the kitchen. From Kaya's end of the conversation and her pale face, he guessed what was happening. He hunkered down to be on eye level with Natalie. He took her hand and drew her to his side.

"You're not feeling so hot, pumpkin?" he asked.

"No, and I don't want to go to the hospital again," she said, her chin trembling.

Kaya heard her daughter's comments as she replaced the receiver. "I'm afraid we'll have to go. Dr. Reiger wants to see you. The good news is that he doesn't think you'll have to stay long."

"How long is not long?" Natalie wanted to know. She was snuggled in the crook of Joshua's arm.

"I'm not sure. It'll depend on what kind of throat infection you have. If it's strep, he'll give you the antibiotics that worked fast the last time." Kaya stroked her daughter's hair. "Come on. We've got to pack an overnight case. We have a long drive ahead of us."

Joshua turned Natalie to look at him. "Have you ever been in a helicopter?"

"No."

"How would you like to fly to Abilene in the chopper?"

"For real?" Natalie asked, saucer-eyed.

"For real."

"All right!"

"Now go and pack what you need," Joshua said.

As soon as Natalie was out the door, Kaya turned to him. "Joshua, thank you for offering the chopper."

"Hush," he said, when he saw the raw emotion in her eyes. "It's the least an uncle can do for his favorite niece." He rose from the chair. "Just how worried are you? Do you know something you're not telling me?"

Kaya shook her head. "No. Just that in her weakened condition, any kind of infection is dangerous."

Joshua saw her clenched hands and the fear deep in her green eyes. "Come here," he said and drew her into his arms. "I guess it's natural for a good mother to worry about her child, but Natalie will be all right." Kaya was as stiff in his arms as if she'd been tightly wrapped with baling wire. "It'll be all right," he murmured against her hair. His hands stroked her back, trying to ease the tension.

"Joshua, please don't be nice to me now or I'll fall apart, and I can't afford to do that."

"I'm here to help you. You don't have to face this alone anymore." She relaxed for a moment and then tensed again, as if she remembered something.

"I'll be on my own again when we leave here in August. It's better if I don't get used to leaning on someone."

"I'm not someone. I'm the uncle of your daughter. Don't you know that from now on I'll be a part of your lives? Do you think I'll forget about you after you leave here?"

"You don't have any legal obligation to help us."

Joshua muttered a four-letter word. He was so upset he didn't even apologize for using it. He took a breath, trying to swallow his anger.

"I know you don't think highly of the Cunninghams. I also know we have a reputation for being somewhat ruthless. There have been times when we've had to be tough and hard to hang on to our land, but we're not without a sense of right and wrong. At least some of us aren't."

Stricken, Kaya looked at him. "I'm sorry, Joshua. I didn't mean to hurt your feelings, and I didn't mean to imply that you're without a sense of morality. I'm just so worried. I'd hoped that Natalie would stay well the entire summer and really build her strength up so that she wouldn't catch every cold and sore throat that hits her school in the fall." Kaya bit her lower lip to keep the tears at bay.

"I know you're worried. But Natalie's going to get the best care money and influence can buy. That I promise you." He heard her take a shaky breath. "Now go and pack what you need. I'll get the chopper ready so we can leave as soon as possible."

"Well, how did you like your first chopper ride?" Joshua asked Natalie as they walked toward the hospital entrance.

"It was neat."

"Kaya?"

"I thought it was a little noisy." In front of her fearless daughter, Kaya wasn't about to admit that she'd been scared the whole time. She'd flown only once before when she'd been sent a ticket to attend her mother's most recent wedding. In the big commercial plane she had been able to close her eyes and pretend most of the time that she was on the ground. She could say one good thing about the chopper ride, though: it had temporarily dulled her anxiety about Natalie.

The nurses on the pediatric ward greeted the little girl like a cherished friend.

Dr. Reiger, informed of their estimated time of arrival, met them a few moments after they'd checked in. He examined Natalie, prescribed medication, reassured them all and told them he would see them in the morning.

While Kaya helped Natalie get ready for the night, Joshua went to the coffee shop for ice cream which Natalie said was all she could possibly eat.

"We've got chocolate and chocolate and chocolate," he announced when he returned, carrying a large paper cup. "When I was a kid, I had to have my tonsils out. The only thing that could get past my aching throat was ice cream. What you do, Natalie," he said, sitting on the edge of the bed, "is take a spoonful, let it melt in your mouth and then let it slide down your throat. You'll hardly notice you're swallowing anything and the cold will soothe the soreness."

Natalie followed her uncle's instructions and managed to eat all three scoops. Even though it was still early, Natalie fell asleep before Joshua finished the story he was reading to her.

Kaya kissed her daughter's cheek before they tiptoed out of the room.

"Now what?" Joshua asked.

"I usually stay with Natalie. The nurses bring a cot for me. How about you?"

"I'll get a hotel room."

"You can stay in my apartment, if you like. No sense in paying for a hotel when there's a perfectly good bed at my place. This is already costing you a fortune."

Joshua shot her a surprised look. "I'd like staying at your place. Thank you, Kaya." He was immensely pleased that she trusted him enough to invite him to her apartment. "I don't know about you, but I'm hungry. Let's get a bite to eat." When she hesitated, he added, "You've got to keep your strength up."

Knowing he was right, Kaya nodded. "All right."

"Where would you like to go?" When she shrugged, indicating that it didn't matter to her where they went, he named several restaurants.

"I'm not really dressed to go to any of those places," she said, glancing at the jeans and T-shirt she was wearing. "But there's a place near my apartment that serves pretty good pizza. Do you like pizza?"

"Love it. Tell me how to get there," he said as they got into the rental car.

The warmth of Joshua's smile caused Kaya to stand up straighter, to breathe easier. His being beside her gave her hope. Perhaps Natalie would get well quickly. She would, if Joshua had anything to say about it! Kaya almost smiled. His optimism was rubbing off on her, helping shore up her flagging strength.

"Thank you," she murmured.

"For what?"

"Being here with me."

"I couldn't be anywhere else."

Suddenly Kaya felt the soft evening air enfold her, smelled the faint scent of the petunias planted in the flower boxes near the entrance, felt the presence of the man beside her like a tangible omen of something momentous ahead of her.

The restaurant was as unpretentious as the neighborhood in which it was housed.

Over the top of his menu, Joshua watched Kaya's every move, her every expression. Even under the unflattering, harsh overhead light, she looked so lovely he couldn't stop looking at her. The arrival of the waitress put an end to this pleasurable occupation.

After they had ordered, Kaya said, "Natalie loves Gino's pizza."

"We'll bring her here when she gets out of the hospital."

"She'll love that. Thank you, Joshua." Kaya smiled at him warmly before she added, "And thanks for bringing us in the chopper. It saved me a long, hard drive."

Kaya looked at him with shining eyes that tied his stomach into knots. He didn't want her gratitude. He wanted her as he'd never wanted a woman before. Subduing his desire, he said, "You don't have to thank me. You're family. Naturally it goes without saying that I'll do everything I can to make life easier for you."

"You're amazing. That kind of spontaneous help and support is what family members are supposed to offer each other, but so rarely do." Kaya reached out to touch his hand.

Joshua entwined their fingers before she had a chance to remove her hand from his. "I know, and that's too bad. People don't usually realize that until they're faced with a crisis. The lucky ones realize it then. Many don't until it's too late."

He looked thoughtful, as if remembering something. From their mutual past? That wouldn't be anything happy. Before he could bring up that old, contentious subject, Kaya said, "You've never mentioned your ex-wife." The astonished expression on his face told her that this was the last topic she expected her to bring up.

Joshua shrugged. "There isn't much to say about Pat. The marriage was a mistake for both of us. The ranch wasn't what she'd thought it would be, and married life wasn't what I thought it would be. She didn't expect the Diamond C to be so isolated."

"And you? What did you expect marriage to be?"

The arrival of their food interrupted the conversation. As soon as the waitress had served them, Kaya repeated the question.

"I suppose I expected a wife to fill the emptiness left by Derrick's death and my father's, but it didn't work out that way."

"You must have been lonely," Kaya said softly.

Joshua was somewhat taken back as if he hadn't considered that before. He nodded. "I guess I was. But I found out that you can be as lonely being married as being single. It didn't take long for us to see that neither one of us was happy, or had a chance of becoming happy in the marriage. So we parted."

"Sounds very civilized and amicable."

"You're surprised. And a little skeptical. Why?"

Kaya shrugged. "I find it hard to believe that a marriage can be ended with so little pain, so little emotion. So...so dispassionately."

"Maybe because there wasn't that much passion and emotion involved in it to begin with."

"You weren't passionately in love with each other? Not even in the beginning?"

"We were attracted to each other when we dated. And we got on okay together. Our relationship was sort of amiable. Sort of bland, I guess. So, not staying together didn't pitch either of us into a deep depression." Joshua shrugged. Looking at Pat had never put him in the same feverish state that looking at Kaya did.

When Joshua saw Kaya's expression, he said, "I can't interpret that look. What are you thinking?"

"I'm trying to imagine a bland marriage. All my mom's marriages have been tempestuous, and Maria and her husband have occasional loud, heated disagreements. Maybe temperamental and cultural differences account for that."

"And the chemistry between the man and the woman." Joshua looked at Kaya speculatively. Grinning, he said, "I can't imagine a relationship between you and me being bland. I can't see you slinking off into a corner to sulk quietly."

"Oh? And you? You'd go off quiet as a lamb? Ha! You've never minced words with me. You've let me have it with both barrels."

"Maybe so, but you give as good as you get. Want to try to see how we'd be together?" he asked, grinning engagingly.

"No, thank you. I have enough problems."

"I'm not trying to take over your life."

"Aren't you? You're so used to issuing orders and everybody obeying them, that you don't even realize how much like a steamroller you are."

Surprised, Joshua realized that there was some truth in her claim. "I'll try to be more considerate. Be more sensitive and understanding."

Kaya laughed out loud. "You couldn't even say that with a straight face."

He grinned back at her. Then his expression grew serious. "What are you thinking?"

"What it would have been like if I had married you instead of Pat." Joshua could have kicked himself for saying this out loud.

"Lily would have had a coronary."

"Odd, that your first thought was what my stepmother's reaction would have been."

"Not so odd. It nearly killed her when I married Derrick. Marrying you would have been the last straw. You underestimate that woman."

"Maybe, but you underestimate me." Softly he added, "More importantly, you underestimate yourself."

Surprise lamed her tongue for a second. "You think I'm a match for Lily?"

"You are now. You'll see that when you face her."

Kaya shook her head vigorously. "I intend to stay as far away from that woman as I can. I don't want her to know about Natalie."

Seeing the panic in her lovely eyes, Joshua laid his hand soothingly over hers. "You don't have to face Lily. I just wanted you to know that I think you're now strong enough to do so."

"If I never see her again, it'll be too soon."

"You're an intelligent, hardworking, sexy, beautiful woman. Why do you have such a low opinion of yourself?" Joshua asked.

"Because other people do. They take one look at me, and see a stereotype. Few bother to look beyond the type to see me." Kaya frowned, trying to find the right words. "I don't have a poor opinion of myself. Deep down I know I'm all right. It's just that this opinion isn't shared by most people right away."

"I looked beyond the stereotype a long time ago."

"You did. I give you credit for that, but the problem is that it didn't matter because you didn't like what you saw."

"That's not true anymore. If it ever was. Which I doubt."

That he'd desired her, Joshua had known, but that he liked her, really liked her, he hadn't realized or admitted to himself. Suddenly he wondered if Kaya liked him. She had no reason to like him. He'd given her a hard time from the moment she'd set foot on the ranch again. He'd had his reasons, and though he hadn't come to terms with her past actions, his anger had cooled—as his blood had heated? He liked Kaya, he desired Kaya, he...Joshua stopped himself short.

Kaya glanced at her watch. "I think you better take me back to the hospital. I want to be there just in case Natalie wakes up."

Natalie responded amazingly well to the antibiotic and three days later they returned to the ranch.

The first thing Natalie wanted to do when they got back, was to see her horse. Joshua gave her a piggyback ride to the corral.

After lunch Kaya put her down for a nap. Looking down at the sleeping child, Joshua said, "She looks pretty good for having been in the hospital."

Kaya nodded. "Children are resilient, thank heaven."

"But you look pale. You've been cooped up inside. Let's go for a ride," Joshua said.

"Now?"

"Why not? We'll be back by the time she wakes up. You know Clancy will be glad to watch Natalie."

"You have an answer for everything, don't you?" Kaya muttered, slanting him a severe look that failed to be convincingly severe.

Joshua grinned at her. "No, but I'm working on it. Come on, Kaya."

"A ride does sound good," she admitted.

"I'll saddle Lady for you. Meet me outside in five minutes," Joshua said and left before Kaya could change her mind.

He took her on a trail she hadn't been on before. "Where does this lead to?"

"Wait and see."

When they reached the top of the rise, she saw the creek. At this time of the year there wasn't much water in it, but the formation of the land had forced its bed to become narrow and deep enough to form a swimming hole.

"It isn't much, but it'll wash the dust off." Joshua wound the reins of their horses on a bush.

Kaya walked down to the water's edge. Kneeling, she trailed her hand in it. It was cooler than she'd expected. She scooped up water and let it trickle down her throat. "This feels good."

"It'll feel even better when you get in," Joshua said, watching the water run down her neck and mold her blouse intriguingly to her breasts.

"Get in?" Kaya looked at him. He was sitting on the ground, removing his boots and socks.

"Get in with our clothes on?"

"Nope." Joshua rose in one fluid move.

"But we didn't bring our bathing suits."

"So? I've seen you in your underwear. Remember?"

She did. Only too well.

"Our underwear is at least as modest as most bathing suits. Probably more so."

He was serious about getting undressed. She watched him unbutton his chambray shirt. The release of button after button revealed the fine, golden curls of his tanned chest. Kaya couldn't take her eyes off him. What was it about the act of unbuttoning a shirt that she found so fascinating?

"Well? Aren't you going to join me?" he asked.

When she saw his hands move toward his belt buckle, she whirled around, turning her back on him.

The sound of the zipper lowering wasn't loud enough to cover his amused chuckle. "I bet you never stuck a dollar bill in a man's briefs."

"What a waste of a dollar bill," Kaya said.

"You know what they say: don't knock it until you try it."

A moment later a big splash told her it was safe to turn around. Kaya saw his head emerge from the water. He shook it, sending water flying in all directions.

"This is great. Come on in." When he saw Kaya hesitate but look longingly at the water, he asked, his voice silky, "Don't those boots feel hot and tight? Don't you want to get your feet wet and cool?"

Maybe she cold just dangle her feet in the water. Kaya took off her boots and socks.

"Is that all you're going to take off?" Realizing how that sounded, he quickly added, "I mean, you must be hot all over. I bet your blouse is sticking to your back. Then there are those pesky flies."

As if on command, a couple of the annoying little beasts buzzed around her face.

"They won't bother you in the water," Joshua added with the finesse of a salesman who knows he's landed a sale.

"Turn around."

Joshua moved his arms lazily through the water.

"I won't come in until you do."

Joshua grinned at her but turned around.

Kaya undressed in record speed. She freed her hair from

the rubber band before stepping into the water, testing it. Then she lowered herself to her knees, letting the blessed liquid come up to her shoulders. With cupped hands she sluiced water over her face and neck. When she stopped and opened her eyes, Joshua was less than a foot away from her.

"Isn't this better?" he asked with a smile. He took her hand and tugged. "Come on in."

"I'm not a good swimmer."

"Don't be afraid. I've got you. You're safe." Joshua's arms encircled her waist as he drew her into the deeper water.

"Put your arms around me. That way there isn't a chance of me dropping you."

She was afraid of the water, and she was wary of him. Fear of the water won out. She clung to him. He loved having her this close. He smiled at her reassuringly.

"No flies. And it's cool. Isn't this better?" he asked.

She nodded.

"Kaya, I give you my word that I won't drop you."

Joshua always kept his word. She took a shaky breath and nodded again.

"Now relax and enjoy." Slowly he turned them, letting the water lap at them in smooth, concentric circles.

His golden lashes looked darker now that they were wet, but his eyes were as deep a blue as the immense sky above. This close, she saw the fine lines radiating from the corners of his eyes. Squint lines from years of outdoor work. She felt an overwhelming urge to touch them, to smooth them. She felt a number of overwhelming urges, all of which she dared not act on.

If she felt only a physical attraction, it wouldn't be so bad. But she liked him, she admired him, and she was beginning to have deep feelings for him. All her emotions where Joshua was concerned were strong: her occasional anger, her desire, her liking. With him she was apparently incapable of moderation. And that was dangerous.

"Hey, you're supposed to be relaxing and enjoying yourself."

"I am."

"You looked as if you were thinking deep thoughts. What?"

"Nothing worth talking about."

"Okay. We don't have to talk. Lips can do other things than form words." To demonstrate, Joshua kissed her, lightly, carefully, tenderly. Then his lips skimmed over her cheek all the way to her ear. His teeth tugged gently on her earlobe, eliciting a small, surprised gasp from her.

"Your ears are lovely," he murmured, "like the rest of you, but you never wear earrings. Why not?"

Kaya looked at Joshua, astonished, that he had noticed something as insignificant as that. "I never could afford really nice ones, and the others..." Her voice trailed off.

He would buy her earrings. With gold settings that would mirror the warm tones of her flawless skin. And with green stones to reflect the vibrant color of her eyes. Then, remembering her fierce pride, he realized he would have to find some convincing pretext to give them to her. Christmas? No, that holiday was too far away.

"Kaya, when's your birthday?"

"Next month. Why?"

"I thought I'd take Natalie to the Crossroads to get you a card."

"That's sweet of you."

He didn't say anything but indulged his desire to look

at Kaya's face. She was so beautiful that the sight of her almost hurt his eyes.

"Joshua, why are you looking at me like that?"

"Because you're so homely, why else?" He could see she was pleased by his teasing words. He wanted to tell her that when he caught sight of her unexpectedly, she took his breath away, that when she touched him, his heart lurched sideways in his chest, and when she was this close, his body was in danger of exploding. He kept these thoughts to himself, afraid that they might spook her.

Joshua had been careful not to let his eyes stray below her chin again after that first look that had sent desire racing through his blood. Knowing her nipples were visible through the wet lace of her bra and knowing how the water caressed her full breasts, he might forget his good intentions.

When Kaya shifted her body and her breasts brushed against his chest, Joshua groaned. Did she know how fragile his control was? When she moved again and gently bit his earlobe, he asked, his voice tight, "What are you doing?"

"Only what you did to me."

"This is like playing with fire," Joshua murmured.

Kaya smiled at him. "Would you say we're in deep water?"

Joshua chuckled. "We're in deep water, both literally and figuratively."

"Then you'd better move us toward the safe, shallow shore."

"This time, Kaya. Only this time."

His husky voice held both a sweet threat and a bold promise.

Chapter Nine

Kaya was fixing sandwiches when Joshua walked into the kitchen. She hadn't expected him for lunch. His arrival caught her off guard. Ever since their afternoon at the swimming hole two days ago, they had tiptoed around each other. Something between them had changed, though Kaya couldn't, or wouldn't, put a name to the change. Now they looked at each other across the width of the kitchen. Since they were alone, Kaya let her mask slip and gazed at Joshua with warm and tender eyes.

He was wearing his working cowboy outfit and looked magnificently fit and all male. She felt a tightness in her chest that caused her to take an extra breath before she spoke to him.

"I didn't expect you for lunch," Kaya said to cover her nervousness and her need.

"Didn't expect to be here, but something came up."

"Trouble?"

Joshua noted the concern in her captivating, beautiful green eyes. Her interest wasn't faked, even though she'd stayed as far away from him as was possible living in the same house. He'd let her keep her distance, thinking that not seeing her constantly might make him want her less. It hadn't. He felt the same hunger, a hunger that distracted him from getting a good day's work done and kept him from enjoying a decent night's sleep. He wanted her with an intensity that in his saner moments shocked him.

"What's wrong?" she asked.

"I took care of it."

"You want a sandwich? I was about to call Natalie and Clancy for lunch."

"Yeah, thanks. A sandwich would be fine." He watched her nod and turn to the counter to make another sandwich. Looking at Kaya did nothing to douse his desire for her. Not that she dressed provocatively. On the contrary. Neither her old jeans nor her faded T-shirt were form-fitting. Yet on her they looked sexy enough to tempt an angel. It was Kaya herself, he realized, the female essence of her, that called to him on every level. She possessed an earthy, eternally feminine quality that drew him to her like a siren song.

Was she aware of her power? If she was, she didn't use it or exploit it. Joshua was grateful for that, suspecting that he'd have great trouble keeping his hands off her if she ever decided to aim that potent weapon at him.

"I have a surprise for Natalie."

Kaya whirled around to face him with a look of dismay on her face. "Oh, no! Not more presents. You promised you wouldn't buy her anything else! She'll get so spoiled—"

"It's nothing I bought, so relax. Besides, a few presents aren't going to turn her into the spoiled little princess you think it will."

"We have to go back to our old life at the end of the month. I don't want you to make that harder for Natalie by constantly giving her things."

"We have to talk about you going back to Abilene," he said.

Surprise caused Kaya to stare at him speechlessly. Finally she blurted out, "What's to talk about?"

"Hey, Mommy, guess what?" Natalie yelled from the back door.

"Natalie, don't shout. I can hear you just fine."

Natalie ran into the kitchen, followed more slowly by Clancy.

"Hi, Uncle Joshua. Are you eating with us?"

"Sure am. Let's you and me go and get washed up."

After Joshua and Natalie had left the kitchen, Clancy spoke. "Did we interrupt somethin'?"

Kaya shrugged. "Nothing but a possible argument."

"In spite of all the time you've spent at the ranch, he still can't understand or accept you leavin' Derrick and the Diamond C?"

Startled, Kaya looked at Clancy. How much did that shrewd old cowboy know or guess? She didn't tell him that the incipient argument would not have been about Derrick. Or would it have been? Neither Joshua nor she wanted to raise that painful subject again, so it still hung between them, unresolved.

Clancy scratched his head. "The fact that he can't handle your leavin' could be partly my fault. We never talked about his mama leavin' the ranch. Not the real reason she left. Ray gave orders that Edith's name not be mentioned in this house. But now he's dead. I reckon that frees me from that order."

Natalie skipped into the room. A minute later Joshua stuck his head through the door.

"Natalie, I have a surprise for you. Close your eyes," he said.

"Okay," she agreed with an expectant grin.

Kaya gasped when she saw the dog Joshua led in on a leash.

He hunkered down in front of Natalie. "You can look now."

Natalie's blue eyes opened and then opened even wider when she saw the dog.

"Hold out your hand for him to sniff," Joshua instructed.

Natalie did. The dog, little more than a puppy, licked her hand. Natalie giggled. "He's so cute. Whose dog is he, Uncle Joshua?"

"Yours, if you like him."

"I like him! I *love* him!" Natalie petted the puppy who proceeded to lick her face.

Before that could get out of hand, Joshua intervened. "Okay. I'll put him on the porch while we eat." When he saw Natalie's disappointed expression, he said, "You can sit with him on the front porch as soon as you've finished eating. Okay, Kaya?"

"That's okay, but has anybody thought about what will happen to the dog when we go back to Abilene?"

"Well, he can stay here on the ranch and Natalie can visit him on weekends. If we can't come up with a better solution."

"Mommy, please say that I can come to visit him. Please?"

"I guess that'll work," Kaya said.

"Well, that's settled." Joshua took the young dog outside. "Natalie, you better wash up again."

When they were seated around the table, Natalie wanted to know all about the dog.

"What's his name? Where did he come from?"

"He doesn't have a name yet, and I got him from our neighbor. Seems he took in a dog named Duke six years ago and this puppy is his descendant."

"Duke? My Duke?" Kaya asked.

"Yeah. I never knew what happened to him." Joshua shot Clancy a telling look. "When I went over to see Ben about the north fence, he asked me if I didn't want to take one of Duke's puppies. Seems somebody from the Diamond C persuaded Ben to take Duke so he wouldn't have to go to the pound or—" Joshua broke off, realizing that Natalie was listening intently.

Kaya blanched. "She was going to…?"

"Yeah, or find a place for him," Clancy added quietly.

"And you found a place for him," Kaya murmured, her voice husky with emotion.

Clancy nodded. "I'm sorry I couldn't tell you, but I had to promise to keep my mouth shut in exchange for finding somebody who'd take him."

"I'd much rather Duke found a new home," Kaya assured him. "Thank you, Clancy."

"A good home," Joshua said, when he saw the wet sheen in Kaya's eyes. "Duke lived until last summer. Ben really liked that dog and took good care of him."

"Who's Duke?" Natalie wanted to know.

"He was a dog I liked a lot," Kaya said.

Natalie wrinkled her forehead. Looking at her mother, she said, "I thought you couldn't have any pets because grandma was 'lergic to them?"

"That's true. Grandma is allergic to pets. Duke was a dog here on the Diamond C."

"Oh." Natalie stuffed the last bite of tuna sandwich into her mouth and chewed, obviously thinking earnestly about something. As soon as she'd swallowed her food, she spoke. "Where's Grandma Cunningham?"

A shocked silence held the adults spellbound.

Oblivious of the impact of her words, Natalie continued. "I know Grandma Swanson is in Germany because step grandpa is in the army, but where's your mommy, Uncle Joshua?"

Because the question surprised him, Joshua blurted out the truth. "I don't know."

"You losted her?" Natalie asked, her eyes saucer-wide.

"More like she lost me," Joshua murmured.

Natalie apparently heard him, for she turned to her mother in alarm. "You're not going to lose me, are you, Mommy?"

"No, of course, not." Kaya stroked her daughter's hair in a comforting gesture. "How could I lose you, or you lose me, when we always tell each other where we're going to be, and when we'll be back, huh? Tell me that, Miss Worrypuss."

Natalie nodded, reassured. "I always know where you are, Mommy. And you know where I am."

"That's right," Kaya added, her voice like an exclamation point. "You want more milk?"

Natalie shook her head. "Can I go out on the porch with the puppy, please? We have to think of a name for him."

"Okay, but stay on the porch." Kaya smoothed her daughter's hair before the girl ran out of the kitchen.

No one said a word until they heard the screen door close behind Natalie.

"Out of the mouth of babes," Clancy muttered.

"I'm sorry," Joshua said to Kaya. "Her question caught me off guard. You know I wouldn't do anything to upset Natalie."

"I know. What are we going to tell her? I know my daughter. Even though she didn't pursue the topic of Grandma Cunningham today because she was eager to see the puppy, she will bring it up again. I can guarantee it."

"Well, she really wants to know about her grandmother. We'll have to tell her about Lily—"

"No! Not yet. She asked about your mother, Joshua."

"Yeah, but that's because she thinks—"

"Stop it, the both of you," Clancy ordered. "It's been my experience that tellin' the truth is best in the long run. Specially when dealin' with kids. We'll have to tell Natalie about Lily. And you and I, Josh, need to talk about your mama. Should have done it years ago, but Ray was muleheaded. Probably felt guilty, too, deep down."

Joshua looked at Clancy as if he'd suddenly sprouted horns.

"Don't look at me like that, boy. She wrote to me. That was after Ray went hightailin' it after you and her and brought you back and got the judge to give him custody of you permanent."

"What?" Joshua's face had lost all color. "What are you saying? My mother took me with her when she left the ranch?"

"Sure did. She loved you, Josh. Still does." Clancy cleared his throat before he continued.

"You was too little to remember, but she wouldn't give you up, not even when Ray stuck the court order in her face. Took two deputies to hold her so Ray could grab you. It was enough to make a man sick. The only reason I stayed on the Diamond C was because Edith begged me to stay to keep an eye on you and to let her know how you was doin'."

"I don't believe this. Any of it. Why didn't Dad tell me about my mother? Why didn't you?"

"I'm sorry about keepin' this from you, but your daddy would have thrown me off the place if he'd known I was writin' to Edith. As it was, he fired me once because I stuck up for your mom."

"I don't remember that," Joshua said with a frown.

"Ray told you I went to see my folks."

"Yeah. I remember now. I must have been in second grade."

"I guess you kept asking about me, wondering when I was coming back, having bad dreams, so Ray swallowed his pride and asked me to come back. He asked real nice, too."

"You said you 'stuck up for Edith'? How?"

"Ray saw her in town. He was going to get the sheriff to run her off. We argued about that. I told him his court order didn't include the town and Edith had every right to be there. He didn't know that she'd come to all school functions and sit in back. After that argument, I warned her to stay away, but she wouldn't. Or more likely, she couldn't. She'd arrive late and leave early, wearin' some ugly old wig, clothes three sizes too big, and thick glasses. Nobody recognized her until you were in seventh grade."

"What happened then?" Joshua asked.

"You started to play football and Ray started to come to watch the games. He recognized her even with her wearin' her disguise. Maybe by the way she walked. Or maybe he heard her say something."

"What did Ray do?" Kaya asked, dreading the answer.

"He threatened to send Josh to a boarding school back East. He meant it, too. Edith knew how unhappy Josh would be away from the ranch, so she swore an oath she'd stay away. She kept her promise, even though it must have broken her heart."

After a long silence, Joshua asked, "But she *did* leave my father when I was baby, didn't she?"

"Yup, she did. Had her reasons. Not for me to say if they was strong enough for her to leave or not."

"What reasons?" Joshua demanded.

"You ain't gonna like hearin' this about your daddy, but back then Ray was wild. Explains where Derrick got his wildness. 'Course Ray was young when he got married. Real young. Maybe too young. But he did get married and that didn't stop him from raisin' heck all over the state. Drinkin' and chasin' women. Edith wouldn't or couldn't put up with that after a time. Especially the other women."

"I can't believe this. Dad wasn't like that at all."

Clancy shrugged. "Edith leavin' and almost losin' you helped settle him down. He grew up some real quick. And later? Well, Lily wasn't the quiet, ladylike type. She didn't tolerate no foolin' around. Kept an eagle eye on Ray all the time."

"All these years. All the lies. All the secrets." Joshua shook his head as if trying to clear it of all he'd heard. He got up without a word and left the kitchen.

Kaya stood up, too, but Clancy laid a restraining hand on her arm. "Let him go. He needs to be alone and think about this for a while.

"Where will he go?"

"Probably for a ride. He'll be back."

"Poor Joshua. What a shock it must be to find out that the mother he blamed all these years for abandoning him, didn't do so. At least not willingly. And poor Edith.

To have her baby taken away like that." Kaya shivered in fear and empathy. "I can't think of anything worse than that."

Joshua did not come back in time for supper. He did not return until Kaya was already in bed. When she heard him enter the house, she put on her robe and went downstairs. She found him standing at the kitchen sink, drinking a glass of water.

"We were getting worried about you," she said.

"No need to. I'm okay."

"I doubt that. You look like you wrestled a demon and lost."

"A couple of steers, but not a demon. And I didn't lose."

"That's very important to you, isn't it? Not losing? Not being wrong?"

"Maybe." He studied her over the edge of the glass. "I have a hunch these questions are leading up to something."

Kaya shrugged.

"Don't stop now," Joshua said. "You got my curiosity aroused."

"Well, you don't like being wrong and today you discovered that you've been wrong about your mother all your life. That's enough to spook anybody, to put it mildly."

"Now why did I know the conversation would end up being about my mother and me?"

"You don't have to get defensive or sarcastic. As important as a mother is in a child's life, how could this conversation not end up being about your mother?"

"Easy. I don't want to talk about her."

"But you think about her. Don't tell me that you don't, because I won't believe that." Kaya studied his face. The set of his mouth indicated that he was not in an approachable mood. Too bad. Kaya wasn't about to let him get away without talking.

"I have some idea how you feel," she said. "Somebody you'd thought very highly of disappointed you. And that's hard. I know."

"How could you know?" he demanded harshly. "Did you find out your father lied to you for your entire life?" Joshua shook his head as if he still couldn't believe it. "Somebody you admired and put on a pedestal deceived you?"

"My father didn't even bother to stick around to lie to me. But somebody I put on a pedestal disappointed me bad, so I know what that feels like. Sort of like having our insides ripped out."

"Yeah." Joshua put the glass down.

He looked so exhausted that Kaya moved toward him instinctively. "Can I get you something to eat?"

Joshua snorted. "You and Clancy. I swear you two think everything can be fixed with food."

"Food is a source of comfort and nourishment. It's almost an automatic reflex to offer that kind of comfort to people you care about. I'll heat up some of the soup Clancy made for supper. You've got to be hungry." She took the soup from the refrigerator and poured it into a pot which she placed on the stove. Seeing him still standing at the sink, she looked at him sternly. "Sit down. This will take a few minutes."

"Bossy, aren't you?" Joshua asked, half exasperated, half amused.

"I'm a mother, remember? Mothers have to be a little bossy. Comes with the territory."

"I wouldn't know."

Kaya heard the bitterness in his voice. Stricken with remorse, she said, "I'm sorry, Joshua. That was extremely insensitive of me. I can't believe I said that."

He acknowledged her apology with a hand gesture and dropped tiredly into a kitchen chair.

Kaya stirred the soup. When it was hot, she ladled it into a bowl, placed crackers on a plate and carried both to the table. She poured each of them a glass of milk before she sat down at the kitchen table. Facing him, she sipped her milk.

Once Joshua stared eating, he devoted his attention to the food. When he'd finished the serving, Kaya emptied the rest of the soup from the pan into his bowl.

"I guess I was hungry without realizing it," he murmured.

Kaya brought the cookie jar to the table.

"Hot soup, cookies, and milk. All comfort foods?"

"I think so. Natalie does, too."

"Clancy was right. You are a good mother. It can't be easy being a single mom, having to earn a living, and taking care of everything. I don't know how single moms do it."

"They do it because most of us don't have a choice. Most of us worry a lot. I already worry about Natalie becoming a teenager." No sooner had she uttered these words, she regretted them. "I shouldn't have told you that. Makes me sound weak."

"You're one of the strongest women I know."

His praise drove warmth into Kaya's cheeks. "Thanks."

Looking at her intently, he asked, "Do you still think I'll try to take Natalie from you?"

"No, not really." She paused for a moment, then looking unwaveringly into his eyes, she asked, "Are you?"

"No. Not unless you give me a reason, which I doubt you'll do." Joshua reached across the table and entwined his fingers with hers. "I hope you're not superstitious about questions dealing with death, but I have to ask you something. Who'd you name as Natalie's guardian in case something happened to you?"

"Maria."

Joshua nodded approvingly. "You should add my name, too. Or don't you trust me enough for that?"

"I…trust you."

Sensing some reservation, he asked, "But? What are you afraid of?"

Kaya shrugged, her expression apologetic. "You might try to spoil Natalie, but hopefully Maria would provide a counterbalance."

"If she's anything like you, I wouldn't get much of a chance to spoil my niece." Pressing her fingers slightly, Joshua added, "Speaking of spoiling, I've been thinking back over the years. You were right. We spoiled Derrick. Lily would have spoiled him anyway, but since he'd been sick as a kid, the rest of us did, too."

Seeing how ill at ease Joshua was admitting this, Kaya felt a flood of warm feelings for him rush through her. She returned the pressure of his fingers.

"You don't admit very often that you're wrong, do you?"

Joshua raised an eyebrow. "'A Cunningham is never wrong'," he intoned. "That was my grandfather's creed. He drummed it into my father who drummed it into me."

"Must be nice to be so sure," Kaya said wistfully.

Joshua shrugged. "If you can convince yourself to believe it."

"You mean you don't? Could have fooled me," she said with a teasing smile.

Joshua raised her hand and bit lightly into her index finger. "You're a Cunningham. You believe you're never wrong?" he asked.

"Heavens, no. But then nobody drummed that belief into my head. If the question of being right or wrong arose, my mother automatically thought I was wrong. To give her credit, she thought that about herself, too. Nothing in our background put us on the side of right. I'd guess it takes several generations of privileged upbringing before you buy into that."

"And even then there are lots of times when you wonder about being right. At least I wonder about it. My dad probably didn't, or he would have told me about my mother."

"What are you going to do about her?"

"Do?"

Joshua sounded surprised. "Do, as in going to see her?" Kaya watched a look of unease and uncertainty chase across his face.

"She wouldn't want to see me. Too much time has passed. I'm all grown up."

Kaya withdrew her hand from his and stood up. She walked around the table until she stood next to him. Joshua stood also, looking at her, clearly not knowing what to expect. For emphasis she laid her hands against his chest.

"If you were my son, I'd want to see you if you were eighty and I a hundred. Don't you know that she's been living for the day she can finally meet you in person? Joshua, that woman has loved you every minute of her life, waiting, hoping that someday she'll be allowed to spend time with you."

"Then why didn't she come to the ranch after my father died?"

"For one thing, Lily still lived here, and she has a reputation for…well, never mind. For another, your mother was probably afraid to come, afraid that you might not want to see her, that you'd reject her. She doesn't know that Clancy finally told you the truth. She still thinks you believe your father's version of what happened. Give her a chance to tell you her side of the story. A woman doesn't leave her husband easily. She must have had her reasons. I think you owe it to her and to yourself to find out what they were."

"Do you really think I should go and see her?"

"Yes. Now you know only part of the truth. You said you didn't like secrets. Here's your chance to learn the whole story." Kaya looked at Joshua beseechingly.

Looking into her pale green eyes, he said, "It's hard to say no to you." He shook his head. "I probably shouldn't have told you that. You could easily take advantage of me."

"That's not my style." Kaya placed her arms around his neck and pulled his face down to hers. She brushed her lips lightly over his, teasing, sipping, knowing that soon she'd taste his mouth fully.

She leaned into him, even as she tried to remember that Natalie was asleep upstairs and that she had promised herself to stay away from Joshua. Telling herself that she shouldn't touch him, kiss him, did no good. She couldn't stop from caressing his fair hair where it touched his collar. It was as fine and as soft as the finest silk.

"This feels so good, Kaya."

Joshua's low, crooning voice flowed over her like a seductive love song. She closed her eyes.

"Kaya, sweet, sweet Kaya, I want you."

The words stopped her. As much as she liked hearing

them, she knew she could not succumb to them. Kaya drew a shaky breath. "It doesn't matter what we want." Her voice sounded trembly.

"We?" Joshua tightened the hand he'd wrapped around her long, glorious hair. "What *we* want?"

"Yes, *we*. You heard me right. I'm having a hard time staying away from you." Her voice was stronger now, even a bit defiant as she admitted her feelings. The look that passed over Joshua's face was one she had never seen there before. Kaya's knees felt as if they'd turned to rubber.

"We," Joshua repeated reverently. "What do you want to do about us?"

"Do?"

"Don't panic. I didn't mean right now, though I'm tempted to toss logic and control clear into the next county." Joshua loosened his hold on her hair. Gently he stroked it into a semblance of smoothness before he spoke again. "I've got to settle a few things first. But I'll be back. We'll pick up where we left off, so remember exactly where we were." He placed a quick kiss on her mouth before he walked out of the kitchen.

Kaya got up early the next morning. Her late-night encounter with Joshua had led to an uneasy, wakeful night. The short stretches of dream-filled sleep she had managed to snag, had left her tired and headachy.

When she entered the kitchen, Clancy was just plugging in the coffeepot.

"You're up early, Miss Kaya."

"Couldn't sleep."

"A lot of that goin' around," he remarked.

"You, too?"

"Yup. And Josh. Matter of fact, he's already gone."

"Gone?" Glancing at the window, she said, "It's not even light out."

"He didn't go nowhere on the ranch."

"What makes you say that?"

"Saw him get into his car, dressed in a suit and tie."

Kaya considered that information. "There's nothing on his calendar about a business meeting. You got any ideas where he went?"

"He left a note on the kitchen table." Clancy pointed to the half sheet of paper.

Kaya read the note, hoping to find a clue in it that explained Joshua's strange departure. In the weeks she'd been on the ranch, he had always told her when he left the ranch. The note said nothing except that he would be gone a couple of days and that Clancy should take care of Kaya and Natalie. She recalled every word they had exchanged the evening before. What if... The glimmering of an idea filled her with anticipation. Carefully she tamped down her excitement. No sense in raising false hope.

"Clancy, does Joshua know where his mother lives?" When Clancy looked at Kaya, his face mirrored her excitement and hope.

"I put the address and the phone number on his nightstand. He couldn't miss seein' it. If he went there..." Clancy rubbed his bewhiskered chin. "Boy, I sure hope he did. Edith deserves knowin' her son. That woman's been through enough heartache to last a lifetime."

"I hope and pray he went. For selfish reasons," she added.

Clancy nodded. "It'll take some time, but Josh'll come around, Miss Kaya. He ain't intolerant, just bullheaded. And he's a Cunningham. Raised to think he knows what's best. Mind you, that's important if you have to run a spread the size of the Diamond C. I know that. But I tried to teach him that everybody makes mistakes, includin' him, and that you gotta forgive mistakes."

"I bet that wasn't easy for him to accept and understand."

"Sure wasn't. Humility and forgivin' don't come easy to most men. And if you've been raised the way Josh was—"

"I understand that, Clancy."

"Just want to make sure you'll make allowances for Josh. He's a good man. One of the best."

"I know that, too."

After pouring Kaya a cup of coffee, Clancy went to the bunkhouse to cook breakfast for the men.

In the silence of the kitchen, Kaya's thoughts whirled and chased each other so vigorously and clamorously that she could almost hear them. They were the same thoughts that had kept her awake for most of the night. She had accepted the fact that she was in love with Joshua. She hadn't wanted to love him, but she was now resigned to loving him, and loving him raised all sorts of questions—hard, painful questions that robbed her of her peace of mind.

They couldn't go on as they were. She knew that, and Joshua knew that.

Did he care about her, or did he only desire her? Did his wanting them to return to the ranch on weekends after school began, promise a future for them, or did he only want to see his niece? Could she remain his weekend lover if he didn't love her? What would this do to his relationship with Natalie, especially once his passion for Kaya cooled?

Kaya shivered, though the morning was already warm

and humid. She could imagine nothing worse than still loving Joshua and having to come to the ranch with Natalie when he no longer even desired her. She couldn't stop loving at will. She had found that out with Derrick. It had taken death and many years before her heart had healed. Oh God, she couldn't go through anything like that again.

Perhaps Joshua was beginning to love her. There had been unguarded moments... No. She must not delude herself with false hope. She would have to wait and see, even though the waiting was hard, so bitter hard.

Clancy's return stopped her fruitless speculations.

"You goin' back to bed or do you want some breakfast?" he asked.

"Breakfast, please. I'm wide-awake. Might as well get an early start on all that work." And stop all her useless worrying.

Three hours later Natalie burst into the den, already dressed, handing a brush and rubber band to her mother.

"Where are you off to so early?" Kaya asked after receiving her morning hug.

"Clancy promised to help me take Prince for a walk. He's not trained yet to walk on a leash."

"Prince?" Kaya asked, brushing her daughter's long, shiny hair. "Is that what you named the dog?"

"Yes. His great-granddaddy's name was Duke, so I named him Prince."

Kaya didn't have the heart to tell Natalie that she had gotten the hierarchy slightly wrong. "Prince is a good name. Gives the dog something to live up to." She fastened the rubber band around Natalie's hair. "There. Have you had your breakfast yet?"

"Clancy's fixing French toast now." Natalie skipped out of the room, her ponytail bouncing.

Kaya smiled. Her daughter's recovery was amazing. Their stay on the Diamond C was working wonders. That alone was worth all the heartache that might descend on Kaya.

She was restless all morning, missing Joshua. Even though he spent hours out on the range, the mere fact that he was on the Diamond C added excitement and anticipation to her day. If this restlessness was a foretaste of things to come once she left the ranch, she was in for a rough ride. She hadn't counted on missing him quite so desperately. She had assumed she would leave the Diamond C and Joshua at the end of the summer and resume her life in Abilene as though nothing much had happened. That was before she had allowed herself to fall in love with him.

Allowed? She hadn't had much choice in the matter. Kaya heaved a deep sigh, hoping to ease the longing in her heart and the uneasiness in her mind. The sigh didn't help. She suspected that the feeling of having a hole in her chest that ached with yearning would only increase, not decrease, once she left the ranch.

Restlessly Kaya walked to the window. The day was sunny and cloudless, so why couldn't she shake this feeling of impending disaster? She was being fanciful. What she needed was some exercise. A long ride to clear her head. Hadn't Joshua mentioned that Lady needed a workout?

Chapter Ten

When Kaya returned from her ride, she saw a four-door sedan parked in front of the house. Visitors for Joshua? She started to unsaddle the horse when one of the ranch hands rushed to help her.

"Thanks," she said with a smile. "Did you see who arrived in that car?"

"Yup. The queen bee herself." When the cowboy realized he was speaking with a Cunningham, he averted his eyes in embarrassment. "I mean it's the old...I mean it's Mrs. Ray Cunningham."

"Lily?" Kaya felt as if she'd been sucker-punched. Shock immobilized her for a couple of heartbeats. Then fear for Natalie sent her sprinting toward the house.

When Kaya burst into the hallway, she saw Clancy hovering just beyond the living room door. He shrugged helplessly, apologetically, and pointed toward the open living room door. Kaya took in the scene at a glance. Lily, wearing an elegant white linen suit with red and navy accessories, presided over a tea tray. Opposite her, Natalie sat in a deep armchair that seemed to swallow her up, carefully holding a teacup chest high with a scared look on her face.

With decisive but measured steps Kaya walked to her daughter's side and held out her hand for the cup. Natalie gave it to her with a relieved, tremulous smile. Only then did Kaya look directly at her former mother-in-law whose eyes were as frosty as a winter night in Siberia. Their glances locked.

"Hello, Lily," Kaya said with a calmness she didn't feel. "I see you have met my daughter, Natalie, who is far too young to drink such strong black tea, but thank you." Kaya set the cup on the tray and stood beside her daughter like a bodyguard ready for action.

"Well, for goodness' sakes. I meant no harm to the child," Lily drawled. "I think it's never too early to teach the social graces."

Kaya felt herself blush, remembering the awkward, humiliating experience of the first time Lily had forced her to pour tea for her visiting friends, criticizing every move in the guise of teaching. It upset Kaya that the incident still had the power to make her feel acutely uncomfortable.

"I remember you teaching me the social graces and hating every mortifying minute of it. But I can live with that. What I find much more difficult to understand are some of the social graces you taught your fourteen-year-old son, including the fine art of making a pitcher of martinis and letting him sample them. He made good use of that skill later in life."

Lily blanched. Then her face flushed a deep, angry red. "Not in front of the child," she said in a low voice. Looking at Natalie with a forced smile, she asked, "Honey, don't you want to go and play for a while?"

Natalie looked at her mother for guidance. With Lily any discussion could easily turn ugly. "Will you excuse us for a moment, Lily?" Kaya took her daughter's hand and led her out the door.

"Clancy, can you keep Natalie safe and out of the way for a while?" she asked with a meaningful look.

"Sure thing, Miss Kaya." Clancy took Natalie's hand and as fast as his lame leg allowed, walked her down the hall toward the back door.

Kaya returned to the living room. Lily had regained her composure. She sat regally in her chair, balancing a cup daintily on her knee.

"I see you wormed your way back into our house," Lily said without preamble.

"I didn't worm my way in. Joshua invited me. And it is his house now, not yours. Now you're as much a guest here as I am. Isn't that so?"

"I wouldn't put it quite like that."

"Joshua did." Kaya watched Lily's eyes widen in surprise before they slitted into a fury-laden stare. Her fingers tightened around the fragile handle of the cup until Kaya feared it would snap off.

Lily subjected Kaya to a merciless head to toe examination. "Are you and my stepson getting…cozy? Is that it? Well, you look pretty good," she admitted grudgingly. Then her expression turned disdainful. "For your type. You've got something that seems to appeal to men. I can't see it myself."

"Can't you?" Kaya asked softly, not allowing the snide tone of Lily's voice to get to her. "I suspect that the 'something' that appeals to men, if there is such a thing, is a quality we have in common, *Lilybelle*."

Lily looked as if Kaya had dumped a bucket of cold water over her carefully styled hair. "My name is Lily, and you and I are nothing alike."

"Not in character or personality." *Thank heaven,* Kaya added silently. "But our backgrounds are very similar. Joshua told me all about you, so you can drop that fake lady-to-the-manor-born attitude."

"Joshua had no right to tell you anything about me!" Lily snapped. Then the corners of her carefully lipsticked mouth turned down derisively. "Oh, I see. You got it out of him in bed, didn't you? Pillow talk."

Although Kaya could feel heat rush into her cheeks, she remained calm.

"My, my. And with my own granddaughter sleeping in the next room."

Kaya wanted to knock the cup out of Lily's hand and wipe that smirk off her face, but she didn't. Instead she retreated behind the old shield she used to put up to protect herself against Lily's barbs. Her face became an expressionless mask. She could not afford to reveal her fears to Lily.

"What makes you think Natalie's your granddaughter?"

"Just looking at her tells me that. And her age. And—" Lily paused dramatically "—Joshua told me."

Kaya flinched, a reaction that wasn't lost on her mother-in-law.

"Joshua told me, and Joshua doesn't lie," Lily said, her voice smugly triumphant.

"He phoned you out of the blue and told you? I don't believe that."

"He didn't just call me out of the blue. Somebody else did. I still have friends in the area. But Joshua didn't deny it when I phoned him night before last."

"Did you tell him you were coming to the ranch today?"

"I told him I wanted to see Derrick's little girl."

"But did you tell him you were coming today?"

"Well, no. What difference does it make what day I came?"

Joshua hadn't deliberately set her up. At least it didn't seem as if he knew Lily was planning to arrive almost immediately. Would he have stayed at the ranch if he'd known his stepmother was coming? Kaya desperately wanted to believe that he would have stayed to help her face Lily. He had as much as promised but then he had also assured her that Lily wouldn't come to the ranch during the summer.

"Natalie sure does favor her daddy, doesn't she?" Lily remarked with a catch in her throat.

"Yes, she does," Kaya agreed with that tenderness that always crept into her voice when she spoke of her daughter. Noticing a possible softening toward her former mother-in-law, Kaya said, "You claimed you wanted to see her. You've seen her." Though Kaya didn't say it, her expression and stance clearly indicated that she thought it was time for Lily to leave.

"You don't believe for a moment that I'm going to settle for one measly visit, do you?" Lily asked, her finely plucked eyebrows raised a fraction of an inch. "Not even you can be that naive. She's the only grandchild I'll ever have. I want her in my life."

"No!"

Something in Kaya's dead-calm voice must have gotten through to Lily for she put her cup down and stood.

"I've accomplished what I came to do: take a look at Natalie to satisfy myself that she is Derrick's child and not a scheme of yours to get money out of the family. But this isn't the end of it. I'll be back. I have a right to visit with my darling grand baby." With that parting shot she turned and walked out the door, careful not to pass within striking distance of Kaya.

Kaya rushed to the window. When the sedan drove away, relief pulsed through her, allowing her shallow breathing to become normal. The relief lasted only for a second. Then the full implication of her predicament hit her.

What she'd been afraid of, had happened. Lily wanted to be part of her granddaughter's life. Exert an influence on Natalie. Kaya shuddered. And Joshua had sold her out. That hurt most of all.

Clancy rushed in as fast as his crippled leg allowed. "I saw the queen bee leave. Are you okay?"

"Yes. No. I don't know." Seeing that he was alone, she clutched Clancy's arm, her eyes wild with fear. "Where's Natalie?"

Clancy patted Kaya's arm reassuringly. "She's fine. She's in the bunkhouse. What's wrong? What scared you?"

"Lily will be back. She wants to be with my baby. I can't let her do to Natalie what she did to Derrick. Oh God, Clancy what am I going to do?"

"First of all, calm down. She ain't gonna do nothin' to our baby girl. Josh won't allow it."

"Don't you speak to me of Joshua! That traitor! That rat! He kept promising me Lily wouldn't find out about Natalie, and the first chance he got, he sold me out. Told Lily that Natalie was Derrick's daughter. How could he do this to me? I believed him! I trusted him." Tears of anger, of frustration, of despair, coursed down Kaya's cheeks.

"Please don't cry, Miss Kaya. I'm sure there was a good reason for Josh to tell Lily. It wouldn't do much good to lie. Sooner or later she'd find out the truth."

"I knew it was a mistake to come to the Diamond C. The place has always caused me trouble and pain. And Joshua—that's the hardest blow of all. He betrayed me."

Kaya's voice broke on a sob, even though she was trying hard to stop crying.

"It might seem that way, but Josh ain't no traitor. He must have had a reason for telling Lily."

"Oh, he did. Punishing me for leaving Derrick. Well, he has succeeded with a vengeance, but I'm not waiting around for the sheriff to arrive with a court order."

"Miss Kaya, where are you goin'?" Clancy followed Kaya down the hall.

"Upstairs to pack."

"Why? You're safe here."

"Safe as a sitting duck, waiting for Lily to come back. No, thank you."

"What are you gonna do? Where are you goin'?"

Halfway up the stairs, Kaya stopped. "It's better you don't know, Clancy. That way nobody can force this information out of you, and you won't have to lie. Please bring Natalie back to the house. Please?"

Reluctantly Clancy left the house.

Upstairs Kaya threw their clothes into the suitcases. She had to get away from the Diamond C fast. For the second time in her life she was leaving this ranch with pain nearly ripping her apart. Served her right for not learning from the first time, she told herself savagely. *And don't you dare cry again.*

"Mommy, why are you packing our clothes?"

Natalie scrunched her face in confusion. Her blue eyes were huge in her face. Kaya hated to do this, but she had no choice. "We have to leave."

"Now?"

"Now."

"But I don't want to leave. There's Prince and Nifty and Uncle Joshua and Clancy and—"

"Natalie, we have no choice. Take that bag of toys and follow me downstairs."

"But you said we could stay until school starts," Natalie wailed.

Kaya dropped the suitcase. Kneeling in front of her daughter, she cradled Natalie's face with her hands. "I know that's what I said, and I'd planned for us to stay until then, but something's come up, and we have to leave right now. I'm sorry."

Natalie started to cry. Kaya hugged her.

"I know this is hard, but we have no choice."

"I'll carry them bags," Clancy said, entering the room. "Mind, I don't like you goin' and I don't think you should. Least ways not until you've talked with Josh."

"I don't want to talk with Joshua," Kaya said in a low voice. Turning to Natalie, she said, "Let's go, sweetie."

Outside, Natalie hugged her dog, weeping into his soft fur. "I'll come back to see you, Prince. I promise I will. I love you."

"That's a sight to break your heart," Clancy said, his eyes moist.

Kaya merely nodded, her heart aching with pain, her eyes filled with tears. She couldn't speak, not even when she gave Clancy a fierce goodbye hug. He seemed to understand. His own voice was gruff with emotion when he told her to drive carefully.

In the rearview mirror Kaya saw him standing there until the bend in the road obscured the house.

Huddled in the back seat, Natalie cried softly. It took all of Kaya's self-control not to give in to tears herself. She kept blinking them away, long after Natalie had cried herself to sleep.

* * *

That night Maria received them warmly and asked no questions until Natalie was bathed and put to bed. Then she filled two glasses with iced tea and invited Kaya to sit in the porch swing. The nearby street lamp shed a dim light onto the porch.

"Out here no little ears can hear what you have to tell me," Maria said.

Wearily Kaya told Maria what had happened. When she had ended the short account, she waited for Maria, who had remained uncharacteristically quiet, to speak.

"Let's hear it," Kaya said. "You obviously disapprove of what I've done."

"No, I don't disapprove, but I wonder if it wouldn't have been better to wait for Joshua to come home."

"Why?"

"Because he could help you with Lily, and—"

"Ha! He's the one who told her about Natalie. He betrayed me! I love him and he betrayed me." Kaya burst into tears. Leaning against her cousin, she wept until there were no tears left.

Next morning Kaya squinted through swollen eyes at the bright sunshine. How could the sun shine and the birds sing when her life was utterly dark? She dragged herself into the bathroom but not even a long, hot shower could work its magic on her. She dressed and went downstairs.

"You're up early," Maria said, studying Kaya's face. "Did you get any sleep?"

"Some."

"What do you want for breakfast?"

"Nothing. I'm not hungry. I'm going to the apartment,

open some windows to air it out, and do some cleaning. Then I'm going to see my boss to find out how soon I can start working again."

"Why don't you take some time off? You told me you saved most of your salary from the ranch."

"I want to keep that as a nest egg. Besides, the sooner I go back to work, the better. I need to keep busy."

"That's not going to make you forget him," Maria said.

"Forget who?"

Maria rolled her eyes. "Joshua. The man you're crazy about."

"I wouldn't say that, but I would say that I'm probably crazy. How else could you explain my falling for another Cunningham?" Kaya lifted her hand to keep Maria from speaking. "Please tell Natalie that I'll be back for supper or sooner."

After washing the dinner dishes, the two women sat again on the front porch.

"Any calls for me?" Kaya had wanted to ask this question since four o'clock that afternoon. The fact that she'd managed to wait three hours pleased her. It demonstrated that she had some control over her life. Yeah, right, some control, she mocked herself.

"No calls. Yet."

"Then there probably won't be any. He isn't going to call. Joshua obviously realizes that he betrayed me."

"No, I didn't."

Both women gasped. Kaya jumped out of the swing and moved a couple of steps toward the porch stairs. Peering through the darkness, she asked, "Joshua? How did you find me?"

"May I come up on the porch, Maria?" Joshua asked politely.

"No, you may not," Kaya snapped.

"Maria?" Joshua asked again.

Ever gracious, Maria asked him to join them.

"Not so fast," Kaya said. "You haven't answered my question."

Joshua didn't stop, forcing Kaya to move back from the top step. "I went to your apartment first. When you weren't there, I knew you'd be here. Natalie told me her aunt Maria's last name, so it wasn't all that hard to find you."

"You wormed the information out of a five-year-old?"

"I didn't worm it out of her. When her aunt and her cousins came up in conversation, Natalie volunteered the last name. I remembered it."

"Now that you've found me, what do you want?"

"You have to ask me that?" Joshua demanded, his voice disbelieving. "Can we go somewhere to talk privately?"

"I'm not going anywhere with you, you Judas!"

"Kaya," Joshua said, clearly trying to hang on to his temper. "I made the long trip back to the ranch and what did I find? You gone again. Can't I leave you without risking you running away?"

"Didn't Clancy tell you what happened? Don't you think I had reasons to run?"

"No, I don't. You—"

"Excuse me, you two," Maria interrupted. "I'm going inside. You can have the porch to yourselves. With the air conditioner running, all the windows are closed so nobody will overhear you. Okay?"

"No," Kaya said.

"Yes," Joshua replied. Facing Kaya, he demanded, "Are you afraid to be alone with me on this porch?"

"Of course, not." Kaya bit her lower lip. "Oh, all right. You can go in the house, Maria."

As soon as the door closed behind Maria, Kaya and Joshua spoke simultaneously.

"You first," Kaya said.

"No, ladies first."

Kaya took a breath before she let the words pour from her lips. "You knew what I was afraid of most. And what did you do? Confirmed to Lily that Natalie was her grand-daughter. And you have the nerve to say that this isn't a betrayal?"

"I didn't know she'd kept in touch with the store owner at the Crossroads. Hattie told her about you and Natalie."

"You could have denied everything. But no! You were only too glad to tell Lily. This was your chance to punish me for leaving your brother."

Joshua's patience snapped. He muttered a string of colorful phrases before he addressed Kaya. "Clancy said you'd made this ridiculous accusation, but you listen to me—"

"Ridiculous? I don't think so. You as good as said Derrick's death was my fault."

"Well, I was wrong!"

That was the last thing Kaya expected Joshua to admit. She didn't know what to say. Mutely she stared at Joshua's face. He looked gaunt with exhaustion.

"I've thought a lot about the past. About everything. If you'd been mine, I would have gone after you, but Derrick couldn't. For many reasons. I didn't see that before, or maybe I didn't want to acknowledge those reasons before because then I'd also have to acknowledge the part I played in spoiling him. And letting Lily spoil him. But all that's in the past. As you said, we can't go back."

"If you didn't want to get even with me, then why did you admit to your stepmother that Natalie was her grandchild?"

"Kaya, do you really think you could keep your secret forever? I'm amazed that none of us learned the truth sooner. Me lying to Lily would only have made her angry. Lying isn't the solution. Don't you see that?"

Kaya shrugged, unwilling to admit the truth of his claim. "But why didn't you tell me she'd called? That's what I can't understand. You didn't warn me and then you left me to face her alone. That looks like being sold out to me."

"I didn't sell you out."

"Ha! Don't even—"

Joshua placed his hand gently over Kaya's mouth before he hauled her against him and kissed her.

At first Kaya was too surprised to resist. Then the sweetness of the kiss flowed through her like a powerful narcotic. This was Joshua holding her. His heady taste, his magic touch, his seductive scent, wooed her into near submission. With the last remnant of her anger, her hurt, Kaya broke free.

"No! Kissing me, making love to me isn't going to make me forget that you betrayed me."

"I didn't betray you. What happened was a crazy, unexpected series of events. I would have told you if I hadn't had to leave in the middle of the night. And I had to leave suddenly because my aunt told me that my mother had to go into the hospital."

This revelation left Kaya momentarily speechless. When she recovered, she asked, "You went to see your mother?"

Kaya's voice sounded much softer, Joshua noted, encouraged.

"And? Don't you dare turn silent on me now, Joshua Cunningham!" She watched him run his hand through his hair.

"I saw her. We talked. It was so strange—a grown man meeting his mother for the first time. She wasn't the heartless witch I'd pictured all those years. We cleared up a lot of secrets and forgave a lot of sins." Joshua walked to the railing and stared out into the darkness.

Kaya followed him. Standing beside him, she asked, "You said she had to check into the hospital. How is she?"

"She had to have surgery. Gallbladder. She came through the surgery just fine. I couldn't leave until I knew she was okay."

"Of course, you couldn't leave. Nobody would have expected you to, but you could have phoned and told me what was going on."

"I thought it would be easier to tell you in person." Turning to Kaya, he said, "I had no idea Lily would hightail it to the Diamond C. When she lived at the ranch, it would take her a whole day just to decide what to pack for a trip. I was sure I'd be back before she arrived. I swear to you that the last thing I wanted was for you to have to see Lily by yourself. You have to believe that."

In the feeble light from the street lamp, Kaya studied Joshua's face. She desperately wanted to believe him. She yearned to trust him with all her heart.

Joshua reached for her and pulled her close. His eyes focused on her kissable mouth longingly.

"Don't even think of kissing me again," Kaya said, but her anger was rapidly leaking out of her. She felt her body leaning into him.

"I always think of kissing you. In the middle of a business meeting, moving a herd, driving a car, in my bed. Especially in my bed. You want to know what I think about when I'm lying in my lonely bed?"

"No!" Kaya was dying to know but she wasn't about to admit that to him. "What I want to know is what we're going to do about Lily. If you found me here at Maria's, sooner or later so will she."

"You're not going to be at Maria's."

"I'm not? And where are Natalie and I going to be?"

"At the ranch where you belong."

"Joshua, be serious. That's the first place Lily will look."

"Let her." Joshua was busy removing the combs from Kaya's hair.

"What do you mean, let her?" Kaya tried hard to ignore his fingers in her hair.

"Can't you be generous enough to let her visit her granddaughter now and then?"

"If that's all she wanted, that would be fine. But I'm afraid it isn't. She wants to have a hand in raising Natalie, in 'teaching her the social graces' which I'm sure she thinks I'm not capable of doing. You didn't hear her. She—"

"Kaya, I know the perfect way to stop her from even thinking about trying to play a major role in Natalie's life. I'm surprised it hasn't occurred to you."

Joshua's voice had mellowed into velvety tones that flowed over her like sensuous caresses. "What way?"

Before he spoke, Joshua slid his hand to the base of her spine. He wanted to feel as well as see her reaction. "Marriage," he said. "If we're married, no one can tell us how to raise Natalie. Not even Lily." He could feel her whole body go rigid with surprise. After several seconds during which Joshua held his breath, she spoke.

"Did you just propose to me?"

"I did."

"Well, that's very noble of you, wanting to marry me to protect Natalie, but—"

"Noble? Hell, there's nothing noble about it. True, I want my niece, but I also want her mother. I've wanted her since the day she reappeared in my life." A look flitted across her face that he couldn't interpret, but it was disturbingly close to being sad. "Kaya, I'm crazy about you. Surely you know that. I haven't exactly been able to hide that." She looked at him silently, wide-eyed. He'd have to prove it to her in deeds, which suited him just fine. He was, after all, a man of action.

He filled his hands with her soft hair before he claimed her mouth, wooing her until she leaned into him, her body pliant, her lips parting to admit him. She was all sweetness and passion, responding to him even as he sensed her doubts. He would erase those doubts. He would make her his, just as he was hers. He kissed her until the kisses threatened his sanity and his control.

"I better go now before this gets out of hand. I'll be back tomorrow. Think about what kind of wedding you want. Sleep tight." He kissed her again, leaped off the porch, and disappeared into the darkness.

Kaya staggered into the house, her heart racing. Quickly she ran upstairs. She couldn't face Maria, couldn't face talking about what had just happened.

Joshua had proposed to her. Unbelievable as that was, it had happened. Kaya stripped off her jeans and blouse and slipped into the narrow bunk bed.

Sleep was a long time coming. Kaya tossed and turned. Joshua wanted to marry her but he had not said the most important words: *I love you*. What was marriage without love? True, she loved him, but that was hardly enough. Or was it?

Kaya tried to think dispassionately, to evaluate her choices and Joshua's proposal. They both loved Natalie. Natalie adored living at the ranch. So did she, Kaya admitted reluctantly. Natalie would be well taken care of. She would receive the best medical care available when she needed it, something Kaya could not guarantee with the kind of jobs she could get. She hated to admit that, but it was the truth.

If she married Joshua, her daughter would have security, the privileges that came with an old, respected name, and an uncle who loved her and would help raise her. Be a sort of father to her. Compared with that, how important was Kaya's selfish desire to be loved? Totally unimportant, she acknowledged humbly. And yet she loved Joshua and wanted him to love her in return. Her thoughts circled endlessly around this problem until finally, mercifully, she fell asleep.

At seven the next morning Kaya heard a discreet knock at Maria's front door. Since the children had stayed up late the night before, Kaya didn't want them awakened yet. She hurried to the door, wondering who could be calling this early.

"Ms. Cunningham? We're delivering your breakfast," a white-uniformed waiter said.

"What?" Kaya asked, staring at the three men carrying trays with silver-covered dishes and utensils.

"Breakfast, ma'am. Where do you want it?"

"This must be a mistake."

"No, ma'am. Where shall we serve breakfast?"

"In here," Maria said, who'd arrived at the door seconds after Kaya.

The women exchanged puzzled looks.

"Who ordered this food?" Kaya asked.

"Mr. Cunningham. He said it was a surprise."

"It sure is," Kaya murmured, looking at the food they placed on the table.

"Thank you," Maria said and walked the men to the door. She found Kaya standing in the same spot she'd left her.

"Wow. Look at that. A bottle of champagne and orange juice. We can fix those fancy drinks. What's their name? Mimosas?"

"Don't ask me. I'm no expert—" Another discreet knock on the front door stopped her words.

"What is this? The Greyhound depot?" Maria opened the door.

She came back with a large, long floral box adorned with a red ribbon. "This is for you."

The exquisite fragrance engulfed Kaya even before she took the lid off. "Oh my," she whispered, lifting one of the roses.

"Joshua must have bought every red rose they had in that store," Maria remarked. She handed Kaya another box. "Quick, open this one. I can't wait to see what's in it."

Kaya removed the red ribbon and the lid. "Chocolates. I never knew bonbons came in so many shapes."

"They even smell expensive," Maria said.

"I wonder what Joshua's up to?"

"A little persuasion, seems to me," Maria said.

Kaya was still in a daze when another knock on the door broke the morning stillness. "I'll get that."

When she opened the door, she found herself face to

face with Joshua. "What, no red ribbon around you? Just about everything else that came this morning was wrapped with a red ribbon."

Joshua grinned at her. "If you'd like me better wrapped with a red ribbon, I can arrange it."

Kaya repressed a grin. "Joshua, what are you up to? What's with all the presents?"

"It occurred to me that I haven't courted you properly. I've never sent you flowers or candy."

"So you thought you'd make up for that all at once?"

"I thought I'd get a start on it this morning. No sense wasting time. About last night. Have you thought about what I said?"

"I've thought about little else."

"Me, neither." Joshua reached into the pocket of his slacks. "Before I forget. I've got one more thing that's wrapped with a red ribbon." Joshua handed Kaya a small jeweler's box. "Open it."

Her fingers were a little unsteady so she had trouble untying the ribbon. When she opened the box, she held her breath.

"Do you like it?"

"It's beautiful."

"So are you." Joshua took the ring from the box. "Hold out your left hand, Kaya."

Wordlessly she complied. When he slipped the diamond on her finger, she said, "You don't have to do all this."

"Wrong! I have to do this. I have to marry you. I swear you've cast a spell on me. I can't survive without you. It's as basic and as inescapable as that." Joshua gazed into Kaya's wide open, warm green eyes and thought he might die on the spot. When she didn't say anything, he added,

"I was going to ask you to marry me before the summer was over anyway. Lily's visit just hurried things along." Joshua raised her hand and kissed it. Then he pressed it against his cheek.

"You were going to ask me to marry you?"

"Of course. I wasn't about to let you go back to Abilene."

"But you never hinted—"

"I didn't want to scare you off before you had a chance to see if you liked it at the ranch. Natalie loves living there and now I'm pretty sure you do too. Don't you?"

Kaya nodded. She couldn't speak. Her thoughts, her emotions, were in great turmoil. "All this is coming at me so quickly."

"I know, but I'm not patient. Love isn't patient. And I do love you."

"What did you just say?" she murmured.

Seeing her surprised expression, Joshua asked, "Didn't I tell you last night that I loved you?"

She shook her head. "I would have remembered that, believe me. You said you were crazy about me, but that's not the same thing as loving me." Kaya wound her arms around his neck.

"I didn't lie. I am crazy about you, but I also love you." Joshua molded her body against his. "I promise to tell you that I love you every day of every year for as long as I live."

Tears of happiness misted her eyes. "I love you, too, and I'll love being your wife." She had to swallow twice before she could continue. "You know the one thing Natalie has regretted more than anything else?"

"What?"

"That she was an only child. She'll adore having a brother or a sister. Or one of each. We'll fill that old house with children and with happiness," Kaya whispered against his lips before she kissed him, pledging her life and her love to him forever.

* * * * *

If you enjoyed what you just read,
then we've got an offer you can't resist!

Take 2 bestselling love stories FREE!

Plus get a FREE surprise gift!

Clip this page and mail it to Silhouette Reader Service™

IN U.S.A.	IN CANADA
3010 Walden Ave.	P.O. Box 609
P.O. Box 1867	Fort Erie, Ontario
Buffalo, N.Y. 14240-1867	L2A 5X3

YES! Please send me 2 free Silhouette Romance® novels and my free surprise gift. After receiving them, if I don't wish to receive anymore, I can return the shipping statement marked cancel. If I don't cancel, I will receive 4 brand-new novels every month, before they're available in stores! In the U.S.A., bill me at the bargain price of $3.57 plus 25¢ shipping and handling per book and applicable sales tax, if any*. In Canada, bill me at the bargain price of $4.05 plus 25¢ shipping and handling per book and applicable taxes**. That's the complete price and a savings of at least 10% off the cover prices—what a great deal! I understand that accepting the 2 free books and gift places me under no obligation ever to buy any books. I can always return a shipment and cancel at any time. Even if I never buy another book from Silhouette, the 2 free books and gift are mine to keep forever.

210 SDN DZ7L
310 SDN DZ7M

Name	(PLEASE PRINT)	
Address	Apt.#	
City	State/Prov.	Zip/Postal Code

Not valid to current Silhouette Romance® subscribers.

Want to try two free books from another series?
Call 1-800-873-8635 or visit www.morefreebooks.com.

* Terms and prices subject to change without notice. Sales tax applicable in N.Y.
** Canadian residents will be charged applicable provincial taxes and GST.
  All orders subject to approval. Offer limited to one per household.
  ® are registered trademarks owned and used by the trademark owner or its licensee.

SROM04R   ©2004 Harlequin Enterprises Limited

COMING NEXT MONTH

#1802 DOMESTICATING LUC—Sandra Paul
PerPETually Yours
Puppy's got his work cut out for him when he meets his new owner,
Luc Tagliano. Though grieving his lost mistress, Puppy wants this
thickheaded human to see how good regular playdates with kind
and patient animal trainer Julie Jones could be....

#1803 HONEYMOON HUNT—Judy Christenberry
When he hears that his wealthy father is globe-trotting with
some new bride, Nick Rampling senses a gold digger's snare and
teams up with Julia Chance, the bride's prim daughter. But their
cat-and-mouse hunt for the couple soon convinces him it's *their*
hearts that are in flight!

#1804 A DASH OF ROMANCE—Elizabeth Harbison
Run out of her catering gig by an evil queen of a boss, Rose Tilden
relocates to a neighborhood Brooklyn diner. But when the handsome
developer Warren Harker shows interest in the area, she learns that
even the chaotic stirrings of love can create intoxicating flavors....

#1805 LONE STAR MARINE—Cathie Linz
Men of Honor
How could ex-marine captain Tom Kozlowski mistake her for a stripper-
gram? Feisty schoolteacher Callie Murphy's anger cools when she sees
the pain in his eyes. And as she reaches out to this wounded warrior,
she's soon wondering if he can't teach *her* something powerful about the
human heart....

SRCNM0106